I0606624

They have to get all the pieces—it's their only chance.

Tim settles onto the couch next to his bag and rubs the back of his neck. "It's perhaps the most important story today. With the Block, we have a chance to find a cure, and you're part of it."

"But I told you, I don't have my section any longer. It's gone somewhere in Latin America."

"I get that, but with all your computer skills, do you think there's a chance you could find it?"

Louis smiles. "You know me, Timmy. I'd do just about anything you'd ask."

"In that case, pour me a scotch, and I'll fill you in on the whole story. We've got to find it."

It's 2020. The race is on to find the cure for a deadly disease targeting women of color. But a hidden side-effect might kill us all. Time to call in the twenty-first-century Robin Hoods to locate, assemble, and decode The Pandora Block.

THE PANDORA BLOCK

John Hegenberger

A Black Opal Books Publication

DEDICATION

For Molly,
Happy Groundhog's Day and Birthday

PROLOGUE

October 10, 1950, Washington, DC:

President Harry S Truman called the air force general on the carpet in the Oval Office. "These operations of yours with Wild Bill have *got* to stop. Don't think we're not appreciative of your detecting firm evidence of the Russian A-bomb test, but we can't have another screw up like that time your balloon device came down in Roswell. All we hear now, even three years later, is UFO-this and UFO-that."

"Yes, sir."

"You're a loose cannon, General. And it stops here and now."

The air force officer held his braided cap tightly under his left arm and deliberated about informing the president of the recent deaths in Turkey. The situation seemed to have ended now of its own accord and was already classified. Better to keep quiet for the time being and not upset Truman any further.

"Yes, sir," the general repeated, sighting above the shorter man's head.

"That's exactly the right attitude," the president snapped and then smiled. "You are dismissed—until tonight's poker game."

The general covered up, saluted his Commander in Chief, and briskly about-faced, knowing that his personal journal contained a full accounting of the disease's outbreak in Turkey.

CHAPTER 1

Friday, July 10, 2020, Trabzon, Turkey:

The sudden concussion blows out part of the concrete wall, twisting the cell door open at the Yildizeli prison to reveal a hallway filled with smoke and flickering neon light.

Jonathan Boyd's ears ring from the deafening explosion that had shaken him from a deep, troubled sleep. In a panic, he claws his way from under rubble to escape the effects of the blast's impact. Hope pounds in Boyd's chest. This Turkish hellhole was never been designed to withstand the assault that must have come from the Russian Aerial Command.

Still groggy, Boyd stumbles up and begins to explore. Cautiously. *Those low-grade drugs they have squeezed into my veins made me sleep through the partial evacuation.*

The entire compound has been taken out during the strike. All around him, walls have crumbled upon both prisoners and guards. An evil gray cloud of chocking dust and ash drifts from a massive blast crater and hangs in the air like a gritty fog.

Boyd limps gingerly on his wounded right leg. Slowly he descends a rickety, twisted metal staircase to the building's half-buried ground floor. He picks his way through the rubble that has been his prison for the last five years.

An armed guard lurches from behind a pockmarked pillar and fires a stream of deadly lead chest-high in all directions from his AK-47.

Boyd drops flat to the filthy ground and grasps a two-foot length of battered steel. *Only one chance.* He throws the metallic fragment along the corridor wall. The panicked guard immediately lets loose with a dozen rounds, targeted where the metal clangs, and Boyd is up, staggering ten feet forward. He crashes into the guard and drives him to the floor. The man's head strikes the concrete with a sickening crack.

Shaken and sweating, Boyd clutches the automatic weapon and fires a round to check that it is still in working order. "I'm getting far too old for this nonsense," he wheezes with fatigue. Patting down the guard's pockets, Boyd finds a mobile phone and a spare clip for the rifle.

Outside, beyond the fence, the sunlight feels wonderfully warm on his face. A shattered I-beam makes good leverage against an abandoned open-top Land Rover tilted on its side. The effort to right the vehicle intensifies the pain in his leg. *Oof!* Boyd's lower back begins to ache. Jumping the ignition and grinding the gears, he navigates across a city gone mad with fear.

The invading Russians appear to have bulldozed their troops four hundred kilometers west in a savage land-grab toward Ankara, the Turkish capitol. Navigating over ruined highways past shattered buildings and distant gunfire, Boyd intends to steer away from danger.

He looks up and sees a haggard face in the rearview mirror. He hasn't seen his reflection, except dimly at the bottom of a water bowl, in over a year. It gives him pause. His features have aged a decade in that time. Hair almost completely gray. Face lined and bearded. Eyes, once clear and blue, now muddy, runny and shocked. A bead of sweat gathers and scrolls down his left temple.

The urge to whisper, "Boo," overcomes him. *Well, maybe not too old.* Boyd slams the car in gear again and drives on, making his way to an estate in the northern sector of the bombed-out city near the Universite Mahallesi, only to discover that the main building is now a pile of smoldering ruins. *Damn!* Boyd had hoped to find someone alive at this sheltered location, someone important, but the military must have already been here and gone.

Now, Boyd searches for and skillfully unseals the safe room hidden beneath the rear of the five-car garage. This was where the art treasures had once been stored. He locates a cabinet of castoff clothing, some stale food, and six bundles of euros, plus a small case containing sixteen small, perfectly cut diamonds. Right where he'd left them years earlier.

A photo of the bearded Iman and gold verses from the Koran embroidered on maroon velvet hangs framed but canted on the cracked wall. Reluctantly, Jonathan Boyd leaves a cache of worn Ottoman coins in their cloth bag. *They're precious, but of little immediate use in this war-torn country.*

The working battery in a tablet computer is of more value, and Boyd takes a moment to coax the device to life. He sends two cryptic messages, praying that the connection holds and the recipients will understand. Are they *even alive?*

From what he'd heard rumored while still in prison, the flood of Syrian refugees had weakened Turkey's position with the European Union. Then an even worse disaster occurred. The origin of the deadly Black Sea Virus was pin-pointed on the county's southern shore. In less than nine months, the deadly virus had forced more than one nation to its knees. During that time, Boyd had heard that panic spread, borders decayed, and the Russians began moving in with a forced occupation.

Boyd knows he'd be extremely lucky if anyone responded to his urgent missives. He leaves the ruined villa and drives south, away from the country's northern shore. Even in a world where tens of thousands are dying, basic daily commerce has to continue. *Mankind is not at an end quite yet, is it? Life still has to go on in the smaller cities, despite the hardship, doesn't it?*

Arriving in the village of Silvas, Boyd spends a few

hundred euros renting a room for the night. He eats the best meal he's tasted in five years at a tiny restaurant. His elbows hunched forward on the bar, Boyd keeps his face shielded from scrutiny with a tan homburg and some-one's cast-off pair of reading glasses. He sits next to a stranded businessman who speaks desperately into a battered iPhone.

A twenty-four-hour news channel plays on a black-and-white television behind the bar. The iKK Kurdish party has joined with the Russian troops. An announce-ment airs from the IOC that the 2020 Olympic Games have been canceled due to fear that the disease might continue to spread during the event. *Who the hell cares?*

Women are dying the world over. In child birth. And so are their newborns. The effects on the Black race are devastating, and the reporter speculates that the BSV might soon infect anyone—everyone. In three genera-tions, human life could become extinct.

Boyd's heart begins to race in his chest. He checks the time displayed at the bottom of the television screen. Six-forty-three p.m. *It's time.* The mobile phone he'd ac-quired from the prison guard starts to buzz.

CHAPTER 2

Los Angeles, United States:

A burly Hispanic intern rolls a wobbly wheelchair out from the front entrance of the hospital. The bright Los Angeles sunshine strikes the passenger full in the face. He winces and then feels fresh pain from the bruises and tightening stitches near his left temple.

Carefully, Tim Cross eases into the back seat of the waiting Honda. *What I wouldn't give for a drink right now.*

Tim had taken plenty of beatings back in the short time when he was a private investigator and even suffered a busted hip playing tackle at USC, but he'd been younger and quicker to heal in those days.

"You going to be okay back there?" Charlie twists around from behind the wheel and, as if reading Tim's mind, offers a can of Coors from a six-pack on the passenger seat.

The reporter pops the tab and slurps the first beer he's had since Wednesday. The foam fills his mouth and goes down easy. "Yeah, I'm fine. Fine as frog's hair."

The balding driver smirks and pulls into the morning traffic on Pico. "You know, the boss isn't going to like this."

"That makes two of us."

"He wants to see you right away."

Cross takes a deep breath and tries not to groan. "That makes two of us again. Can we stop at my place, so I can get a clean shirt?"

"Sure." Charlie's voice sounds concerned. "Give you a chance to get your story straight, too."

Tim stifles a belch. His editor will want to know the truth before the story goes live. It isn't a big story, but it is all Tim has. *This time, Winters surely will have to take me seriously.*

Thirty minutes later, Tim has made himself reasonably presentable and is riding the elevator up to the eleventh floor of the *Gazette* building, where the boss awaits.

Winters is shouting at the phone console on his desk. "Get me that update on the Black Sea Virus and bring it to the editorial meeting in ten minutes." He doesn't look happy. *He never looks happy.* He paces the room, gesturing for Tim to come sit on the worn sofa beside the metal desk. On the opposite wall, CNN plays on a flat screen with the sound off. Some sort of political rally or press briefing in Paris.

Damn, is that Miko standing before the cameras?

"Cross, how many times am I going to have to tell you?"

"What?"

"We're not the *National Inquirer*?" In his late fifties, Winters wears his sleeves rolled up and his tie loose. He is over-weight and over-worked. "The world's going to hell, and you're screwing around with local politics."

Tim dry-washes his face. "You don't get the shit kicked out of you unless you're onto something important, boss. This story could go all the way to the City Council."

"I don't *want* to go there." Winters slumps in the chair behind his desk and runs his fingers through thinning blond hair. "Not without solid proof, anyway. All you've got is supposition and bruises. We need facts, remember?"

Tim can't resist watching his old girlfriend as she speaks before the assembled press in France. Distracted, he responds, "But it is the truth, Mark. I know it."

Winters jabs the remote at the TV screen, clicking the image to black. "Well, I don't. And neither does anyone else. Stick to the assignment Ed gave you and stop giving our paper a bad name."

Tim stands up, trying now to dominate the conversation. "Don't you *want* the truth?"

The boss rises to this full height and leans over his cluttered desk. "Look, Tim. You've been a good investigator for us, but if you keep this up, I'll reassign you on the Home and Lifestyle section. Hear me?"

Without thinking, Tim threatens, "You're afraid of the backlash from City Hall, aren't you? Where's your courage?"

Winters glares and charges around past the reporter to open the office door.

Oh, shit. Tim realizes that his last remark might have gone too far.

"Ed!" The glass in the door rattles as the boss's voice echoes into the room beyond. "You'd better come in here." He turns and stares again at Tim until an older man has eased into the office.

Ed Tompkins—the only person Tim knows who still smokes a pipe. The sweet scent of Cheery Blend floats across the room as the dapper editorial director moves to take up a station next to Winters.

Uh-oh. It immediately dawns on Tim what is about to happen. "Now, wait—"

Winters goes back behind his desk. "We're going to have to let you go, Cross. Ed will help you clear out your cubical. I've warned you before about not following orders. We don't have any more time for infighting or insubordination."

A wave of panic rolls over Tim, making his knees weak. He is being rejected and suddenly feels a loss for words.

"Sorry, Tim." Ed smiles weakly. "I tried to cover for you, but the boss—"

"The boss is fed up." Winters' voice is sharp. Stinging. "I'll send an official notice to the Union, but you'd be smart not to fight it."

Tim's anger seethes. *Fight it? Hell, I welcome it.* "You wouldn't know a good story if it bit you."

"Is that a threat? Ed, here, is my witness."

"No, it's not a threat. It's a statement of fact. No respectable reporter will want to work for this dying rag. I'm not the one who's through here. You are. I'm going over to *The Times,* and they'll be glad to publish my exclusives."

"Then get your ass out! Now," Winters growls between clinched teeth.

And that is that.

When Tim arrives back at his apartment with the banker's box of his office possessions, he considers turning on the TV news. Instead, he pours a stiff slug of vodka and glares down at the sink.

The neighbor's cat has followed him into the kitchenette. Tim feeds the animal the remains of a tuna sandwich, after brushing off a few ants from the crust. The food disappears, and the purring calms Tim's temper. So does the vodka.

He slumps in a wobbly chair next to a rickety table where his laptop sets. The windows on the computer's screen are loaded with reports of riots in Cape Town, South Africa, and the Russian invasion of Eastern Europe. An email icon blinks for attention, and a message pops open when Tim taps the screen.

RECALLED TO LIFE
90-1-287-884-9098
05:44 GMT 072220

"I'll be damned," he mutters to the cat. "Boyd's out of prison. The devil's escaped." *Could this day get any worse?*

Tim switches on a wire-frame fan in an attempt to combat the day's growing heat. He calculates that five-forty-four GMT meant ten-forty-four AM his time. *That's only ten minutes from now.*

At first, he hesitates to make the call. Boyd's the last person, he wants to talk to. It had been Tim's testimony that had led to the thief's arrest. Miko had never forgiven him for turning the man in. But it would have been different if Boyd had been honest when recruiting them for his team of operatives. Instead, the man had lied and turned them all into thieves.

Tim had been suckered into the crime and vowed not to let it happen again. Yet, as the designated time for the call arrives, his investigative instincts lures him into tapping the number into the phone and speaking to the man he'd betrayed five years earlier. "What do you want?"

"I'm sending you money to join me at the estate in St. Croix." The old man's voice sounds weak and out of breath. "I've contacted Miko, too. You have to convince her to come and bring her part of the block."

Tim feels his throat tighten. His palms become damp around the phone and glass of vodka. "I haven't seen her in years. I mean, I've seen her. She's on the news almost every weekend, what with Birol's involvement with the virus, but we haven't spoken since—" He realizes he is babbling.

"Calm down," Boyd insists. "You two are like family. And you hold part of the key to the cure. Get on a plane and bring her with you."

The cat nudges Tim's ankle. "I don't have a family anymore."

"Listen to me, Cross. I know it won't be easy, but you owe me. And this is your chance to get back into her good graces. Maybe your only chance."

It would be satisfying if Miko were to forgive him for "going over to the dark side." Tim discovers a tender bruise below his right ribs where he'd been kicked the day before.

Considering my current career circumstances, a little travel is down-right appealing.

He swallows another mouthful of straight booze. "Send me the money, and I can be there in a few days."

"And you'll bring Miko?"

"I'll—I'll try."

"Bring your section of the Block, too."

When the team had broken up just before Boyd's in-carceration, each member had taken a piece of a bronze cube as a memento to be used to identify one another in the years down the line. It was a criminal fancy, but Tim had liked it and kept his T-shaped piece in his sock draw-er, next to his grandfather's dog-tags. "I'll see if I can find it, but—"

"It's extremely important. Lives are at stake."

Boyd's flare for the dramatic hasn't dampened.

The kitchen fan oscillates, rattling briefly like an an-cient alarm clock.

"Just send the money to my account," Tim advises, ruffling the orange cat's ears.

"You can depend upon it, Cross."

After the call ends, Tim's head starts to ache again. He spends a good fifteen minutes tracing Miko's personal data to find a cell phone number. He then shoos the cat back into the hallway, takes another stiff drink, and gathers his courage before placing the call.

CHAPTER 3

Paris, France:

The reporters shout in a dozen languages.

They're out for blood. Miko Wade firmly grips the podium that supported an ugly cluster of microphones. *Yes, they smell blood in the water all right and are ready to strike. Especially that bitch from* La Monde.

Miko has fenced words with her before back when Birol initially purchased the SpaceZ Corporation. That interview in early 2018 hadn't gone well. Everyone had thought that the billionaire was buying the high-tech company as either a grab for publicity or a tax write-off. But his ballsy management style eventually made a success of the struggling aviation firm, merging it into other sections of Kalic's multinational concern and proving the nay-sayers wrong.

Miko had thrown herself into those long days and sleep-wrecked nights which were necessary to convince the press that SpaceZ could offer the world affordable exploration above the Earth. The new frontier for real this time. Her hard work had paid off. The positive spin had held for over a year before the first fuel tank crash which started the feeding frenzy all over again.

Now, after twenty minutes of intense interrogation, the assembled print and electronic media are still shouting for answers and Miko is their main target. Already the *La Monde* bitch is clamoring, "Do you deny that the crash into the Black Sea was the cause of the viral outbreak?"

Miko Wade takes a deep breath and tries not to let her anger show. "There's no proof of that." She looks straight into the cameras. "And, I'll remind you all that Birol Kalic has already donated more than two million dollars to help find a cure."

"But, isn't that just a cover up?" calls out a France-Twenty-Four interviewer in excellent English.

Miko almost completely loses her composure. "That'll be all, thank you. The press conference is over. Again, thank you all for coming and for your fair coverage."

Leaving the insistent crowd behind in the main ballroom of the George V, Miko returns to her suite on the sixth floor, unconsciously running her tongue around her teeth. It is a mannerism she finds she often falls back on after giving out a series of lies. Her mouth tastes dry and acidic. Miko hated confrontational scenes.

It is too easy to go off message and say something the press will pounce on. *Perhaps they'll all calm down tomorrow.* Somehow, she didn't think so.

Her job hadn't been this difficult five years ago when she'd first come to work for Birol.

In 2013, he'd been riding a tsunami of success, meeting daily with corporate executives, heads of state, and media celebrities. His increasing influence had been one good-news story after another, and the man had rewarded her with financial increases and lavish gifts. *Perhaps, too lavish.*

Miko squeezes the bridge of her nose and strides to her room's wet bar. She pours a couple of fingers of scotch over ice into a crystal glass and takes a full swallow to ease her nerves. Her fingers find a bowl of cashews.

Bing.

Her phone glows with a text message in her private account.

RECALLED TO LIFE

She takes a slow, ragged breath. "Shit!"

જ

At precisely seven-thirty-two p.m., Paris time, as she steps from the hotel room's shower, Miko's phone begins to buzz. It is Tim Cross.

"Tim, how'd you get this number?"

"Um…hi, Miko. Unlike you, I'm still an investigator—of sorts."

"What do you want?"

"Boyd contacted me—"

"Me, too. So?"

"I—I know. He says he needs us to come to the villa in St. Croix and bring our pieces of the Pandora Block."

Her mind flashes back to the image of Jonathan Boyd being taken to a Turkish prison years ago. *The thought of the man still makes my heart quicken.* "Why would he contact you, instead of me? Especially after what you did to him."

"Why? I don't know, Miko. I think he must have escaped. There's insane disorder throughout Turkey from the Russian invasion, maybe even anarchy. And that's on top of the devastation from the BSV. What matters is that he says we can find a cure, if we meet with him."

"That's completely crazy." She begins to picture Tim's dimpled chin as she furiously towels moisture from her hair. "I'm settled in here with Birol and have a million things on my schedule." Even to herself, she sounds like a child talking back.

"Miko, it won't be easy, but you know you have to have the courage to do what's right."

She abruptly hangs up on him, vowing not to do anything he's asked. She immediately blocks his calls and goes back to dressing for the evening's dinner at the Tour d'Argent.

Birol Kalic arrives at her suite without security a little before eight o'clock. He's wearing his trademark broad-shouldered blue suit with gold cufflinks and yellow tie. He acts like the US President come to court a voter.

They share a drink together and the news of the day. Miko decides not to mention the call from Tim. She hopes to completely forget it soon.

Birol loosens his tie with his large manicured hands and tells her that their plans have changed for the evening and they will order dinner in. "It's raining fiercely. And, as you say, the press is out for blood. We will have no peace outside this room, so we'll spend the night here together."

Ugh. Miko hides her surprise and disappointment. "A rainy night in Paris with one of the richest men in the world. How can a person resist?"

"Yes. You'd be a fool to resist." He comes to her with wet eyes like zinc nails and a crooked smile, reaching up to the low neckline of her gown, tugging at the cloth as if to cause it to part. His eyes seem fierce and almost too large. Miko steels herself for what she knows comes next.

Later, in the shadowy bedroom, she slips from under his arm. Alone, in the dim bathroom, her mouth tastes bitter. Again. Her thoughts return to the time, years past, when she'd been an adventurous thief with Tim. Unbidden, the thought spawns a vision of the blue sky and turquoise waters off the coast of the Virgin Islands. *Recalled to life.*

CHAPTER 4

Sunday, July 12, 2020, St. Croix:

Jet-lagged in one-hundred-plus degree, muggy weather, Tim climbs down the ramp of the twin-engine jet from Miami, squinting and rubbing a kink from his stiff neck. His blue-tinted sunglasses do little to darken the bright rays of the Caribbean sun, but at least they hide a few of the dark bruises around his eyes.

He carries his ruck sack through the cement-block Rohlsen terminal usually cluttered with rum sellers and trinket hawkers, but now nearly empty except for a few shifty-eyed baggage handlers and general loafers. The BSV has taken a strong toll here on the American protectorate island. Few people, it seems, want to be out and about where the disease can spread.

Tim's mock t-shirt immediately begins to dampen from the humidity as he flags down a battered taxi, hoping it might be air conditioned. *Of course, it isn't.* The heavy-set black driver chews gum which makes his accent even harder to understand, but Tim finally gets him to repeat the address he wants.

The breeze from the cab's open window is a slight relief. Tim shrugs out of his rumpled travel vest and pulls at the collar of his shirt to try and cool down a bit. The taxi bounces along a rutted two-lane road past a large, abandoned refinery and over the island's main mountain ridge to arrive twenty minutes later at a stone-walled estate on the northern shore.

There is a squawk box next to a keypad beside the closed, iron gate. Tim presses the button on the speaker and announces his arrival. A tiny camera high on the trunk of a palm tree within the compound swivels to inspect him. A mechanical voice tells him which keys to press, and soon he is shuffling his scruffy Nike's up a gravel drive to a broad rambling single-story villa.

Here, at last, he finds blessed cool air. He also finds Boyd, when an armed guard leads him into a sun-drenched kitchen. The lean man, salt-and-pepper hair brushed back and goatee trimmed around his wide mouth, stands at a wooden counter chopping carrots. Boyd wears gray slacks and a rough cotton shirt, its light blue sleeves rolled up to expose tan sinewy forearms.

Tim leans against the door frame. "How'd you get out?" *You old S.O.B.*

Boyd looks up with his classy smile. "I was lucky."

"I've heard that those Turkish prisons are hell, even before the invasion."

Boyd chuckles, scooping up the diced orange disks and adding them to the shredded lettuce lying in a clear glass bowl. "And I've heard that you're a reporter now. That will be useful as we investigate the cure I have a lead on."

Tim's brows lower. *He has a cure?* "Does the World Health Org or the CDC know?"

Boyd moves to a small breakfast nook, setting the bowl in the middle of the red checkered tablecloth. "I'm afraid that it's too fantastic for them." He pulls out a chair and motions Tim to join him. "They'll never believe it, especially coming from me."

Tim settles into a kitchen chair opposite Boyd and sets his ruck sack on the floor next to his feet. "What is it?"

"I'll fill you in later." The elder man grinds pepper into the salad bowl. "Do you have your section of the block?"

"Right here." Tim pats his travel bag. "Why do you want it?"

Boyd holds out a hand, palm up. "Let me see it, please."

Tim finds the T-shaped object and hands it over without a word. *This ought to be interesting.*

Boyd studies it, smiling. Then he reaches into his trouser pocket and brings out a second section, touching the two pieces together. "Yes. Look how the encryption on the edge lines up with that of my piece."

"So? Do you have a drink around here?"

Boyd gets up and finds a half-full bottle of dark rum.

"If we had all the pieces, we could read the full inscription."

Tim pulls the cork from the green bottle and takes a long swig. "The world's going nuts, and you want to play archeologist."

"From what I've been told, this is the key to stopping the virus and the bloody insanity it causes."

"And here I thought I'd heard every kind of wild conspiracy." Tim indulges in another sip of fruity booze. "What exactly are you talking about?"

Boyd sits again, leans back, and stares for a moment out the window as a yellow humming bird darts past. "To be honest, I've never liked you, Tim. You're the last person I should trust, since you're the main reason I was in prison, but we haven't any choice. We have to work together now."

Tim clears his throat. *The moment of truth.* "Sounds like one of your old cons, to me."

"Blunt and to the point. But wrong." The tiny bird swoops away into a bougainvillea bush. "We have to get the team back together again, starting with Miko." Boyd nibbles a small lettuce leaf.

The movement of the man's lips and beard reminds Tim of a pet rabbit he'd owned while growing up in Ohio. "I told you that I called her, but I doubt that she'll cooperate. She hates me for turning you in and has started her life over again."

Boyd pops a bit of carrot into his mouth. "She'll cooperate."

Tim blinks. The rum is still strong on the back of his tongue. "How can you be sure?"

"Because I'm already here." Miko's voice carries ahead of her from the villa's living room.

Holy crap! "Then this must really be important if you've left your billionaire breadwinner."

She hears him, of course, and takes her time to casually step into the kitchen, wearing a silk Hawaiian blouse tied at the waist. Tim notices a hint of cleavage under the blue, red and yellow palm-tree design. Her white shorts hug her hips with a thin brown leather belt that matches her sandals. Clear hazel eyes that bore down on Tim. "I told Birol that I needed a vacation to recharge my mental battery. He didn't like it, but..." She shrugs, and Tim admires her elevated chin.

Boyd has risen upon her entry. "Can I have your section of the block now?"

Miko's neck stiffens. "I don't trust either of you. Tim's a traitor, and you're a cheap crook."

Tim holds tight to his bottle. "Nice to see you, too, after all these years."

Boyd tilts his head. "I must say that I resent being classified as cheap."

"And I was never a traitor, missy." Tim comes unsteadily to his feet. "I did what I had to do for both our sakes. He conned us into joining his team and stealing those art objects, and you well know it." *In fact, I think you liked it.*

Boyd rubs a hand over his goatee. "That's not important now. It's...ancient history. Like the cube. We always thought it was just another intricate work of art in Birol's collection, but it's much more. Let me see your piece, Miko, please."

She stares at him, stifling a slight laugh. "I know you, Jonathan. You have deception in your blood. Shouldn't Interpol or Europol be searching for you?"

That was a bit cruel, but I have to agree. Tim raps the tabletop with his fist. "Here, here."

"And yet, you both came anyway."

Miko's subtle perfume reminds Tim of spring in the Sierras. *That calls for another swig.*

"Take it." Miko thrusts out a hand holding a bit of old bronze. "We all kept our sections as mementos from our time with you. God knows why."

"Unless the others have lost theirs," Tim mumbles. "Or they're dead." He checks his watch. *The return flight isn't for another five hours.*

Miko ignores Tim's negative comment and speaks instead to the older man who studies the metal section. "It's all that's left from the burglary that *this* bum told the authorities about so they could put you in jail."

"And *you* know that it was the right thing to do," Tim quickly responds. "We talked about it."

"No, you did the cowardly thing, Tim." Miko turns her full attention to him. "You quit or wanted to back out because of simple fear."

Boyd raises his voice. "Stop it, both of you. Again, look how the inscription aligns. That's why we have to work together. If I'm right, this could put an end to the virus."

If you're right? Tim's voice goes up an octave. "You really don't know what you're talking about at all. Do you?"

ↄﬡↄﬡ

Cape Town, South Africa:

Thousands are dying. The government is in chaos, with martial law in some parts of the city and riots in other sectors. Everyone wears a mask to dampen the spread of the disease. Bottled water is nearly worth its weight in diamonds. Religion is no relief. The rich flee to Antarctica where the cold is thought to forestall the outbreak. Many people throughout the continent believe that the entire dark race has been targeted by the virus. There is talk of declaring a fanatical war on the other people in the world.

The twenty-year-old sister-in-law of Hank Jones is writhing and screaming in pain. The baby is already dead, and the doctors are struggling to keep her alive if possible. Only a saddle-block injection of anesthetic can relieve her pain. And then only for minutes before the virus takes her.

Hank bites down on his thick lower lip and tastes blood. He tries to recall a Coltrane sax number from the *Blue Trane* album to distract him from the horror that now surrounds him. It doesn't work.

CHAPTER 5

Christensted, St. Croix:

The sun begins to set behind the green mountains, and a sea breeze cools the day.

"Yes." Miko leans in and takes up a piece of carrot. "What *are* you talking about?" *The old man is up to something. But what?* "What's this all about, Jon?"

"Yeah," Tim pipes up. "I'm getting interested, but impatient."

Boyd drizzles red wine vinegar into the salad bowl. "Then shouldn't you cancel your return flight?"

Tim gulps. "H—How did you know that I'd switched to an earlier flight out?"

"I still have a few friends here in high, as well as low, places. Glad to see that you're interested, considering the amount of rum you've consumed."

A blaze flares in Tim's eyes, like lightning in a mirror, Miko realizes.

Boyd smiles again, but *his* eyes remand serious. "I'll answer all your questions—if you two stop arguing."

A lime-green gecko scampers diagonally up the outside wall.

Tim yawns. *Okay. We can play his little game.* "First, I need another drink."

Miko can't help smirking. "What a weakling you've become."

Tim shrugs. "You're partly to blame—"

"That's enough!" Jon Boyd snatches up the rum bottle, almost spilling the last of its contents on the tile floor. "You're both acting like children."

Miko takes a settling breath. *Okay, take it easy.* "Go on. Explain why we're here."

"That's better." Boyd nods. "Do either of you remember Kultar? Yilmaz Kultar?"

Through the French doors that lead to the terrace, Miko catches sight of a new column of black smoke rising from a fire that has broken out somewhere in the city. It is a dark reminder of the insanity surrounding them.

Tim draws his chair in closer to the table and leans in on his elbows. "Kultar was Birol's old art curator, right? He went to prison, too, like you, for some sort of embezzlement." Then he turns to Miko. "Your billionaire benefactor saw to that, while the rest of us managed to get away."

Boyd lets a few fresh mushrooms drop from his hand into the bowl. "Yilmaz and I spent time together on rare occasions when our jailors hosed down and inspected our cells. In addition to being an authority on antiquarian art, he was a bit of a nut about Atlantis."

Miko notices Boyd's use of the past tense.

"That old tale?" Tim takes a pull from at the rum bottle. "Now I'm really interested!"

"Preposterous." Miko hooks her thumbs into the pockets of her shorts. "You're as crazy as he is—or was."

Boyd tightens his expression. "Yes, was. He died of kidney failure, they said. But he knew we had taken the Pandora Block. That single Greek word was the only part of the inscription thought to be translatable."

"I remember," Tim muses. "And the rest of the carving on the bronze cube was gibberish. Some old language long forgotten or never encountered."

Miko hears the wail of a distant siren. *Something's going on out there.* The column of smoke had faded into the evening sky. "Or just plain gibberish to begin with. What's your point, Jon?"

Boyd seems to blush above his beard. "You're right. I didn't believe it at first, either, until the Black Sea Virus struck last year. Kultar claimed that it had happened before in ancient times and that the block described an effective cure."

Tim continues to muse, almost as if Miko and Boyd weren't in the room. "I thought that Atlantis sank into the ocean. What's that got to do with the disease?"

Miko quickly adds, "I think Homer was the origin of the Atlantis myth. He put the lost civilization on a continent somewhere in the Atlantic Ocean."

She glances out at the blue ribbon of the sea and surf.

"I'm convinced now that it wasn't only a myth." Boyd seems assured as he dips a mushroom cap into a splash of dark vinegar and gobbles it down. *They're starting to buy into the whole deal now. Don't blow it.* He swallows and goes on. "And it wasn't located in the Atlantic, either. It was in the other direction, closer to where Homer lived, to the east of Greece, in the Black Sea. And that's our connection to the virus."

Miko feels her heart skip, but she accepts an offered mushroom from the enigmatically grinning thief.

೧౨೧

Busan, South Korea:

On board the medical research ship where he's been at work now away from his family for more than fifty hours, Jae Kim tears off his cloth facemask and strips away the blue rubber gloves. *God, I wish I had a cigarette.* He settles instead for gnawing on his lower lip.

An announcement in his native language blares from the squawk box on the bulkhead out in the companionway. The approaching storm has turned nasty. Preparations are underway to abandon ship.

The vector for the disease is still unknown. And pregnant women are dying every day. At least they aren't members of my own race, Jae Kim thinks with relief. *At least not yet, anyway.*

He has administered to more than a dozen black

women, all of whom have bled out in terrible pain. None of his team of bio-researchers has a solid methodology for halting the lethal virus. With luck, they could succeed in making airborne and thus possibly contained, but only within a controlled lab. Out in the real world, its deadly effects will continue to spread and even flourish. *The chance of spillover is enormous.*

An alert comes onto Kim's cell phone. The North Koreans are threatening to launch a missile attack in the next three hours. The message is chilling. If they target Tokyo, a new world war will undoubtedly ignite within hours

Jae Kim finds the last of a pack of cheap Korean cigarettes and sits in the lab, waiting for results. He discovers that he's drumming his fingertips. He shakes his head, blows smoke, and feels the deck tilt ever so slightly as the ship lists to starboard from the force of an approaching storm.

ↄﬤↄ

St. Croix:

"What a bunch of bullshit."

It is a stunning vindictive, since Boyd had never heard Miko curse before.

"No." Tim leans forward, his right elbow almost tipping the rum bottle. "I'm still intrigued. Go on."

"It *would* be bull shit, I suppose, but the virus has struck near the Black Sea before, back in the 1950s."

Miko remains skeptical. "Then why doesn't the CDC know of it?"

Tim shots back, "Who says that they don't?"

"Because—" Boyd takes a breath, hoping to continue to control the conversation, if not the situation. "—because it was hushed up, since the USA was at the root of the outbreak back then."

"This is dynamite stuff," Tim declares.

Boyd wasn't sure if the reporter was referring to the island liquor or his story. *With Tim, it's hard to tell, even when he's sober.*

The reporter adds, "Your story is so incredible, I may never need to drink again."

Boyd knows better than to believe that.

Miko scratches the side of her face near the thin gold band looped under her left ear. "So, how do *you* know, Jonathan?"

A gray pelican sails past the window, gliding on a Caribbean breeze.

"Of course, you know that Jonathan Doe Boyd is not my birth name." The self-declared buccaneer reaches out to pick up a small book from the kitchen counter behind him. The faded cloth cover is red with small black lettering on the spine. "This journal was written by my great-granduncle Albert. It's a personal account of his involvement with the 1950 outbreak and its subsequent cover up."

"I'm getting lost here." Miko eases down to sit at the remaining chair in the breakfast nook. "I suppose you also have a birthmark on your right buttock that proves you're the rightful King of Bohemia."

It's Boyd's turn to scowl. "I've missed your dry wit."

"No, I get it!" Tim shifts his face from Boyd to Miko. "Jon's saying that the journal describes…" He loses his train of thought. "What, exactly?"

"All right. Let me back up a bit. In 1949, my uncle led a secret operation where the US Air Force flew planes from a base in Turkey and other locations to try and gain evidence that the Soviets had detonated an atomic bomb."

Miko and Tim exchange questioning glances.

"Planes flew out at night and 'sniffed' the air over Russia, bringing back trifling radioactive particles which would prove that a bomb had gone off deep in the Siberian wastes. They found the proof and President Truman exposed the USSR's activities, which was the beginning of the arms race. But one of the sensor planes went down somewhere in the Black Sea.

"So…" Cross lets the word stretch, until Miko Wade adds, "What? I still say that this is bullshit from an escaped convict."

"A con from a con?" Tim smirks.

Boyd continues despite the reactions of his small audience. "The journal says that the downed plane caused the release of a small bubble of gas long held underwater and that within a day of the release, symptoms like those of the current BSV appeared along the northern coast of Turkey. Certain women died in child birth. The government and military did all they could to stop the spread, and, eventually, the outbreak died down weeks later. No one knew exactly why and the whole thing was classified, except for what Uncle Albert wrote here." He taps the book on his open palm.

"And what does all this have to do with the Block?"

Tim jumps in. "Don't you see, missy. It means that there's a cure for the virus. We should—hell, we *must* investigate this."

Boyd is relieved now that they are beginning to understand. "Which is what Kultar claimed was—or is—inscribed on the Block. He was certain that the disappearance of Atlantis corresponded to the original spread of the disease and that the Block had been created to record the cure."

Miko still isn't completely buying it. "Then why wasn't your uncle's outbreak just as deadly? Why wasn't everybody wiped out back in 1950?"

Tim hands the empty bottle to Boyd. "It's a stretch, I know, but if the people of Atlantis were almost killed thousands of years ago, it makes sense to me that they'd want to record the cure for future generations, right?"

"That's the reporter in you talking, and it still doesn't answer my question."

Boyd realizes that they were missing the point. Again. "What if the recent crash of Birol's SpaceZ rocket into the Black Sea released much more of the deadly gas?"

Tim hums. "And caused the new outbreak of the virus that is wrecking the world."

"Bull," Miko responds, then, more slowly, adds, "Shit, you might be right!"

"Exactly." Boyd spreads wide his hands, resisting the

temptation to applaud. "And that's why we must gather the missing sections of the Block and decipher its full message."

"When you say it like that, it sounds easy." Tim shakes his head. "But the CDC is never going to believe this."

Miko seems to be thinking out loud. *Has she finally understood?* "If each of our old teammates still has their sections, we could contact them, put the thing together, and maybe figure out the cure."

Boyd feels a wave of triumph. "We have nothing to lose and the world to gain."

Unfortunately, he is exceedingly wrong.

CHAPTER 6

Calcutta, India:

Birol Zeheb Kalic feels the pressure as the thirty-gauge needle injected the bevacizumab directly into his left eyeball. *Nasty stuff.* He grudgingly recalls that this is the ninth treatment he's endured in the last year to halt the growth of his wet macular degeneration. Will this latest injection finally seal the hole growing at the back of his retina?

The ophthalmologist with the bad breath irrigates the billionaire's eye, removes the lid speculum, and adds a drop of antibiotic. "You should rest now," the diminutive physician advises.

Doctors always say that.

As usual, Birol tells him that he doesn't have time to rest.

"If the treatment is not successful," the dark Indian

eye doctor rambles on, "we'll have to seriously consider the implantation of the mini-telescope prosthesis that we discussed last month."

Birol leverages his bulk from the medical chair, puts on his prescription sunglasses, and prepares to leave the tiny clinic. "And risk completely losing my eyesight entirely? No, thank you."

He should never have allowed himself to be exposed to those radiation bursts during the SpaceZ power system tests. But, like most setbacks throughout his long career, he damn-well wasn't going to let it stop him from ultimate success.

The primary phone buzzes in his coat pocket. *The calls never stop.* He slips into the back seat of the Buick limo. As the car carefully pulls into the heavy Calcutta traffic, and Birol holds the device to the side of his round head. "Speak."

"We've set up another press conference, as you've ordered, sir, but the room is swarming with dozens of camera crews."

"Typical."

"Er…yes," the voice of his junior publicist almost fades from the weak digital reception. "We've been able to control the crowd. Unfortunately, they are growing more aggressive. They want answers now about the next rocket launch."

Of course, they did. "Miko will handle it."

"If you recall, sir, she's on leave for personal reasons."

Birol grimaces. He should never have approved her

sabbatical. He barks an order to locate and bring her back.

"Sir, we can proceed with the launch, if the funding becomes available. The EU wants us to focus more on the problems spreading on Earth, instead of the Mars landing."

"I know that, you fool. Why do you think I'm meeting with the North Korean delegation about additional financing?"

The line goes quiet.

The billionaire realizes that his growing headache has caused his tone to sound threatening. *A couple of pain pills would help. Or a stiff drink.* He takes a deep breath and watches the sea of traffic outside his limo flow past like a school of angry barracuda. India is awash in poverty and unrest. Staging the landing platform out in the Bay of Bengal was beginning to look like yet another bad decision. But the rare earth elements from the mines in north country were essential to success. *Where the hell is Miko?*

"Tell the press that I'll be there to speak to them in twenty minutes. After that…"

"Yes?"

"Never mind." Birol ends the call and lifts his sunglasses to test his vision. Wavy lines still cause the tops of buildings to lean down upon him.

He is the chief-executive officer of a vast financial empire that stretched from Asia and across Europe over the Atlantic. His personal wealth is estimated at well over a hundred billion dollars. His conglomerate, engaged in a multitude of scientific and high-tech programs, is known throughout the globe, yet here he sits, his own vision steadily and progressively continuing to weaken.

Clinching his jaw, he commands the driver to speed up and ignore the crowded streets. "Don't worry. They'll get out of our way." Under his breath, he swears, "The world is going to hell, and my security chief is on a god-dammed holiday."

℞℞℞

St. Croix:

Boyd sits alone in the living room. The deck of cards in his hands is new and stiff. He shuffles them, trying to manipulate the ace of spades, palming it behind his right hand. *Steady.* It holds there for a second. *Steady.* Then it springs away unintentionally, spinning halfway across the room, as a sharp pain stabbed the base of his thumb. He gets up from the sofa and walks into the bathroom to find his arthritis pills.

When he comes back to the couch and coffee table and again picks up the cards, he can overhear the quiet voices of Tim and Miko from in the kitchen. He can tell from their conversation that she is again checking messages on her phone. *I'll have to learn how that is done.* He remembers using Google and Wikipedia, but iPhone apps, Facebook, and this other thing, Twitter, are a series of new mysteries.

Miko clears her throat. "He's right. It looks like

there's some truth to his story. There were minor reports of an outbreak back in 1950."

"This is going to make a killer story," Tim answers, almost sounding gleeful.

"Your choice of words is a little dramatic, don't you think?"

"Hey, I'm a professional writer, and this plot is thickening and twisting quickly."

"And that's another terrible choice of words. You just love uncovering these secret, classified stories, don't you?"

No response at first, then Tim's chair scraps back as he must be getting to his feet. "Did you know that within the CIA's Black Ops organization, there's another, more clandestine team?"

"Let me guess. Nobody can see or suspect them, so they're called White Ops. Right?"

"Oh, so you've heard."

"We need to get some high-powered people involved in what Boyd's proposing, Tim."

"What?" The young man belches. "Like Birol's goon squad? He'll just take over and dominate everything. No thanks."

They are so quiet for a moment that Boyd thinks they have perhaps gone out the back door onto the terrace.

Then, Tim says, "So, are we going to talk about it?"

"You mean about us? No. That's over."

Another short pause, until Tim asks, "Then what about Boyd's plan to find a cure?"

"I'm looking it up now. But it's still fantastic."

Boyd riffles the deck. The card's edges are sharper than he remembers.

Tim's voice carries through the doorway: "Atlantis? Who cares if it's Atlantis or some other old country? It's the idea that the inscription could lead us to a cure that's important. Don't you want to find a cure?"

"That's an obscene question, Tim. Of course, I do."

"Do you know a better solution?"

"No."

An armed guard steps into the living room from the front entrance and bends to whisper into Boyd's ear. What he says is cause for concern, but the timing is terrible. Boyd hesitates to act. Instead, he nods, gesturing for the guard to leave. Then he shuffles the cards again and continues to eavesdrop.

"Let's go get the others and find the sections, so Boyd can—"

"Can what?" Miko still sounds angry.

"That, I don't know. But, it sure is one hell of a story. Do you think there's any more rum around here?"

"If the pieces are assembled and if we can translate this inscription, what happens, then?"

"I don't know, Mik. There's only one way to find out. Let's go with this for now and see where it takes us."

Boyd smiles. *They're coming around to my way of thinking.* He continues to fan the deck of cards and practice his manipulations, awkwardly.

Miko's voice carries from the next room, with alarm. "That's the same attitude that got us working with Boyd to begin with."

"If you'll remember, we both agreed to join the team back then."

"Yes, and I guess we'll both agree to this, too."

"I'm glad to hear you say that."

That's his cue. Boyd rises and enters the kitchen. "So am I. And I want to thank the two of you for coming today. We have our work cut out for us."

Miko gives him a sideways glance and goes back to thumbing her phone. Tim leans back in his chair, running his fingers through his hair. "This is serious business, so I need another drink. You got any beer?"

Boyd steps over to the refrigerator and brings back a cold can, handing it to Tim.

"Ha, ha," the kid says, holding up the root beer. "You're ruining my buzz."

The sharp sound of rapid gunfire outside the house brings them all to their feet.

Boyd opens a drawer and lifts out an automatic. "Right now, we have a much bigger problem."

CHAPTER 7

Miko's heart races as she shoves the phone into the pocket of her shorts.

Boyd opens a door off the kitchen and gestures down a flight of wooden stairs. "My guard's tell me that there is martial law now in the city and people are beginning to riot."

The rattle of continued gunfire causes her to jump. *Holy Crap!* She looks at Tim, who grabs his rucksack and dashes down the steps. Miko doesn't hesitate to follow with Boyd bringing up the rear.

She runs past a series of cupboards loaded with can goods and plastic jugs full of...*What? It has to be fresh drinking water.* The dim overhead lights illuminate what appears to be exotic exercise equipment and a rack of bicycles. Boyd's island residence, it seems, is prepared for a disaster like an annual hurricane, but probably nothing like what is happening now. *Best to stay near him, if she hopes to survive.* There is no time to see anything more, since Boyd rushes past her, down a narrow passage that ends at a short series of steps. These lead up to a concrete structure capped by a metal hatch.

Once outside again in the daylight, the trio bends low, continuing to scurry across the lawn, past a clump of rose bushes. The sky is smeared with gray smoke. They round a high stone wall and Miko's foot snags on a tangle of weeds, sending her down on one knee. She catches herself, palms scrapped and burning.

A four-second burst of automatic fire rips the weathered stone wall above her head. The sound is like some sort of fierce mechanical saw. *My God! They're shooting at us!* Stone chips rain down on her head and back.

Almost simultaneously, Boyd returns fire.

Tim pulls her up by one armpit. "Are you hit?"

She shakes her head, gasping, as if she's been under water.

"Come on," Boyd shouts, moving through an opening in the wall.

Another hail of bullets whizzes past. Back beside the house, one of Boyd's guards covers their exit with rapid fire, and Miko sees an attacker spin and fall from a stuttering impact.

Seconds later, the three scramble into a waiting Volvo driven by another uniformed guard. This one has long greasy hair that droops over his collar. As the car with its panicked passengers grinds into gear, Miko, at last, finds her voice. "This is definitely *not* something I expected to step into!"

"At least, not this soon," Boyd replies.

"Oh, come off it, Mik," Tim huffs. "You love excitement."

Breathless, her heart pounding, she growls, "I don't love being shot at. Keep your head down!"

Tim's only response is a nervous laugh.

He's an idiot. And this is insane!

Miko prays that her hands wouldn't shake as she glances back through the rear window, and then slides low in the seat. Two men with raised rifles are charging around the opening in the shoulder-high wall.

"Step on it, Thomas," Boyd shouts at the driver. The Volvo lurches forward down the inclined dirt road. "Take the back way out and head for the airport." He clamps a hand on the driver's right shoulder, as if to steady the man.

Someone's gray-stripped cat skitters across the roadway. The driver swerves.

Miko swears they are going to crash. But the car jostles and shifts over a series of ruts until it breaks free with a sharp turn onto a paved highway.

Shielding her eyes, Miko finds Tim's arm pressed against her right leg. *Hands off, hot boy.* She gives him a look, but his attention is still trained on the rear window. He calls out, "I think there's another car coming behind us."

Boyd leans around to see over the top of their heads. "Speed up," he instructs Thomas.

Their car accelerates, but Miko can see another vehicle catching up at a rapid rate. Dark smoke continues to spread across the sky. St. Croix is an American protectorate, but now it seems more like a third-world country.

The vehicle pursuing them grows into a navy-blue pickup truck. Frantic, Miko watches its battered grill and front bumper surge forward to ram the Volvo's trunk. She pushes her knuckles into her mouth when she sees the truck pull alongside and slam into their left rear fender. She slides down to the floor and grabs the back of the seat for support. There is a screeching roar as the passenger window above her head shatters into a laminated-crystal downpour.

Both Boyd and the driver return fire from their handguns. *Jeez, the sound is deafening.* Thomas spins the wheel. A bullet must have struck him, because his revolver tumbles up and over the seat to land at Miko's knees. She instantly understands what she must do. Lifting the fallen Beretta, which seems to weigh a ton, she freezes for a second. *This is a lot harder than Hollywood makes it seem.*

Before she could take a breath, Tim wrenches the gun from her grasp and without hesitation begins firing out through the broken window.

The truck lurches to its left and skids off the road into a gully.

Tim smiles with relief for a second and then vomits out the side of the car. Miko holds her own stomach as it begins to heave.

"Thomas has been hit," Boyd calls out to her as the pace of their vehicle slows. "Take over driving,"

The car comes to a stop. Miko swallows deeply and

rushes to change seats with the driver. There is a crimson streak and small puddle of bright blood on the floor next to the accelerator pedal, but she forces herself to ignore it.

While she guns the engine and the car surges forward, Boyd taps Thomas's phone to call ahead to the airport. She hears him trying to arrange for medical care and a flight on a small private plane.

Tim mumbles from the back seat. "If we get out of this, I'm going to swear off drinking for at least a month." Miko recalls hearing that Tim had been undergoing analysis. Maybe she'd been too harsh on him. *Worry about that later.*

Following Boyd's directions, they arrive at a grassy airfield near the shoreline. Near the turquoise ocean, Thomas is transferred to a long white ambulance that looked like it had driven out of the 1950s. Boyd gives the driver a brief hug and pat on the unwounded shoulder, handing him a wad of currency.

The growl of a single-engine plane taxiing in their direction makes Miko realize how desperate their situation had become.

"Come on," Boyd shouts. "We should be able to make it to the next island, if we hurry."

She glances around, feeling that somehow this had to be another of his tricks. *I'm not falling for this.*

More gunfire echoes in the distance. "I'm not going," she announces, shaking a pointed hand at the little aircraft. "Especially in that tiny thing."

The line of Boyd's mouth tightens while the plane rotates around to align itself along the runway.

Tim nudges her hip and shoulder. "Don't be stupid, Mik. We have to get out of here."

Boyd steps on the wing's foothold and opens the passenger-side door.

Miko stands her ground, but Tim nudges her again. "Stop it," she flares.

The sound of gunfire grows louder. Nearer.

Tim raises his gun—in her direction. "Get on the plane."

Boyd holds out a hand to help her board.

Tim's eyes are steady. *Is the gun growing bigger?*

The plane's engine revs, and Boyd shouts, "Now, you two. Now."

She seriously thinks about taking the firearm away from the brat but finally swallows her wrath and climbs into the plane.

⌘

Paris, France:

Sandrine Lecombe spoons the last of the creamy, crunchy profiteroles between her red, dainty lips. The dark chocolate and vanilla ice cream feel cool on her tongue. The day is hotter than she'd like, but she doesn't let it interfere with her mood.

Sandrine sits at a sidewalk table in front of *Les Deux Magots* and studies the little man in the three-piece suit. A trickle of sweat runs down the side of his hawkish face. His lapel carnation had started to go limp even before he joined her at the infamous *resto* just off the Boulevard Saint Germain.

Think I'll needle him with another direct question. "When can you be ready?"

She is disappointed to watch Gerard Garni calmly tap his lips with a blue paper napkin and adjust the glasses on his pointed pink nose. "We are prepared to go anytime. But Tuesday would be best, it being Bastille Day and all. Few will notice us then."

His accent is Armenian, of course. Sandrine recalls once playing the piano at a concert near the musical water fountains in Yerevan. That was the time they had stolen the Ararat rubies together. "*D'accord*. I'll be at the Louvre tomorrow night at two o'clock. Don't let anything go wrong."

"Have I ever let you down?" The man signals the waiter for *l'addition*.

A sudden breeze catches the brim of a wide hat worn by the aging woman at the next table. The gay chapeau skims into the street, where a passing motorist crushes it under the tires of his motorcycle. A girl seated on the back of the *moto* waves as the vehicle buzzes away.

Sandrine brushes aside a strand of her long red hair and shakes her head. "Just like that, Gerard. Even your best plans can still become playthings of happenstance."

CHAPTER 8

St. Croix:

Miko shakes her head. "This never would happen in Paris or Los Angeles."

"Yes, but the rest of the world is not as shielded from the crisis." Boyd gives her a stern look, like a college teacher. "We're going to have to go to even more dangerous places than this to gather the sections from Jae Kim, Sandrine Lacombe, and Louis Nakai."

Tim says, "Ugh, Featherstone," while fingering the Berretta.

Above the humming of the plane's engine, Miko gestures with her chin. "And put that thing away, Timothy." The nitwit tucks the gun into his pants pocket. *Perfect. Next, he'll shoot off his nuts.* "For the record, I'm still not buying the Atlantis stuff."

Tim shrugs. "Well, after all this, we definitely deserve some answers. Don't you think?"

She well knows what to think, but she isn't going to let them know it.

"And we'll get them, I assure you." Boyd nods. "I didn't expect things to be this bad this close to the States."

Miko's attention is drawn to the waters below them. She has flown a great number of times before in a small aircraft, but never this low over miles of open ocean. The vast expanse of dark blue appears chilling, and the small tattered waves far below seem like tiny icebergs.

The single-engine plane hums along, occasionally tilting slightly as the pilot course-corrected.

Miko finds that her palms were damp. She whips them against the seatbelt and yawns repeatedly to clear her ears. *Where the hell are we going? When'll we get there?*

The twenty or more dials and indicators on the control panel don't seem nearly enough to keep them all safely in the air. She wishes for the streamlined jet that Birol always travels in. *Instead of this vibrating toy.*

A sudden gust from the port side of the craft shutters the seats. Tim gives out a laugh like a kid on a roller-coaster ride.

Miko's throat feels warped and uneasy for a moment. She concentrates on swallowing excess saliva.

After ten or fifteen minutes, a dark smudge begins to grow on the forward horizon. *Land at last.*

Boyd turns and taps the back of her hand, pointing.

"We can reach the cruise ship once we land in St. Thomas."

Miko and Tim exchange questioning looks. Boyd has already turned back around to stare confidently at the approaching green and brown landmass.

Despite everything, she can't help remaining attracted to the older man.

Back in the day, he had been the only person who'd recognized her yen for adventure and escape. Boyd had brought her and Tim into his inner circle and trusted them with his clandestine operations. It had been almost as thrilling as heavy sex.

Now, she is letting him take charge again, leading them this time into something unknown, yet exhilarating.

"I have zero luggage now," she shouts, as the plane banks for a landing on the wide, short runway that stretches to the island from the Caribbean Ocean.

Boyd glances back with his bright, unnerving smile. "I'll see if I can have your bags located and sent to your offices in Paris, but don't hold your breath."

"At least, we got away with our skin intact," Tim observes.

Miko hypnotically watches the runway streak under them. "The world is coming apart faster every day."

"Which is why—" Boyd answers, "—we need to act. And act now."

Is this really happening? Miko wonders. *Are we really the only hope there is?*

༄

Boyd recognizes the five-decker cruise ship floating in the harbor outside the small town of Charlotte Amalie, as the plane approaches for its landing.

Once again on solid ground, he and his two companions rush through the bright sunlight and into the cavernous terminal filled with panicked travelers. Armed guards wearing black coveralls and blue berets, carrying AR-47s with banana clips, patrol the gates and passenger areas.

For a second, it's as if he's walked back into the Turkish prison where he'd spent the last five years. His throat tightens, and he feels the faint tingling sensation that always accompanied the closing of a trap. This time, however, his presence seems to go un-noticed.

He has hidden his gun in a jacket pocket, but it burns there now as if white hot when one of the guards came toward the three travelers. A brief discussion with the sharp-eyed official confirms what they already knew—St. Croix is under attack, possibly by what the guard describes as "suspected pirates."

"Well, we're here now," Tim hisses. "Not much chance of going back."

"I didn't think there was." Miko turns her attention to Boyd. "What do you want to do now?"

He thinks hard for a moment. *They're dependent on me now.* "We go forward, Miko Wade. You must travel back to Paris and get Sandrine's section of the Pandora Block. I've got a way to find Kim in Korea, but it's going to be a touch tricky."

"I'd like to help, too," Tim says. "But I can't travel outside the States without a valid passport."

"I'll see about that later," Boyd assures him. "In the meantime, you can track down your old pal, Louis, in New Mexico."

The kid grimaces. "Again, I say 'ugh.'"

Boyd has the impression that Tim can make a joke out of anything in almost any situation. *But maybe that can be useful.* "We need to move fast," he tells both Miko and Tim. "Try and check back with me in the next couple of days. Use the number I gave you."

"Be careful," Miko directs her words at the boy.

Tim cocks a smile back at her. "Because you care about—"

"Because we can't afford for anything to go wrong." She almost stamps her foot. "Remember, we need *all* those sections to find the cure."

Boyd notices that she is definitely coming around to his point of view.

Still smiling, Tim purrs, "Easy does it, eh?"

"This is more serious than a heart attack," she snaps.

"That's funny coming from you."

Boyd lets himself swear. "Christ. Will you two stop arguing?"

Tim's expression relaxes, and he straightens his shoulders. "You're right. Let's go. And good luck."

Boyd thinks that perhaps he'd underestimated the boy, after all. *Time and events will tell.*

They conclude their plans and Miko makes a few phone calls that clear her and Tim for ticketing and boarding a plane back to Miami. She still has skills and influence, which was why Boyd chose her for the task.

Feeling somewhat relieved, he watches as their jet accelerates down the runway and takes to the sky over the sapphire water. He had always been a survivor with backup plans and contingency arrangements, but now he knows he would sacrifice it all to get level again with the world. Without conscious thought, he utters, "God speed," and heads out of the terminal to grab a taxi.

The cab driver gets him to the harbor within ten minutes, but the cruise ship has already departed. *Damn! More threats of pirating, probably.*

Boyd confirms this when he questions a knot of locals at the docks. There is a chance that he could hire a boat and sail after the ship, but even for a high payment, he can find no one in the tiny harbor who will overcome their fear and risk it. And, eventually, too much time has passed, and even a fast speedboat will not be able to get him to the ship. *The world is indeed changing, rapidly evolving into an unpredictable environment of paranoia.*

Not letting his disappointment show, Boyd grabs another taxi to return to the airport terminal.

Alone, during the short ride, his thoughts drift back to the enormity of what he has planned and his chances of pulling it all together. He hopes Miko and Tim will follow through with their assignments, as they have promised.

Despite their past differences, he feels that Tim Cross is intrigued enough to contact the young computer wiz, Nakai as scheduled and retrieve the Navajo's section of the Block.

Miko is another matter entirely. Her current association with the Turkish billionaire is essential to the plan's success, but Boyd senses that the woman is still skeptical about the story of the ancient virus. *Who wouldn't be?* He isn't one-hundred percent sure that even *he* believes it. Still, he wants to believe that there is a cure for the world's troubles and that he can be the one to find it and gain back his respectability. Maybe even a modicum of honor. What he hasn't admitted to the others, and partly to himself, is the desire to make amends for his family's involvement with the earlier outbreak. Maybe he'd never tell them the full details, but the urge to do so is powerful. And that urge, coupled with the drive to exact vengeance on Birol for his years in that filthy prison, drives Boyd to attempt a long-game caper probably beyond his aging abilities.

Once, years ago, he had led a team of thieves for grand personal gain. Once, he had persuaded them to join his band of "Bishops." It had been a brazen chessboard fantasy that felt justified and even heroic back then. But now, could he pull it off again? Or was he too far re-moved from this new, high-tech world?

Nonetheless, perhaps millions of lives are at stake now. Revenge, sweet as it could be, will simply have to wait. Knock it off, he silently scolded himself. *None of that actually matters, considering the threat that the virus poses.*

Boyd arrives back at the airport entrance and cautiously, reluctantly slips his gun under the front seat of the taxi. He takes his place in line at the security checkpoint.

He hopes that the others will do their parts. He knows he needs their knowledge, understanding, and skill sets, in order for his plan to succeed.

Now, he needs to contact Jae Kim. And to do that, he needs to get to Korea.

CHAPTER 9

New Mexico:

The next morning, after his red-eye flight from Miami has touched down at Gallup Municipal Airport, Tim staggers into the one-hundred degree heat and hails a cab for the Burning Rock casino.

He recalls riding through this dusty town back in 2000 with a handful of scruffy bikers on their way to Los Angeles. It had been an act of his rebellious youth in protest against his mundane home-life growing up in Central Ohio. And he had gotten the crap kicked out of him when the other bikers jumped him outside San Bernardino one night and stole his possessions.

But before that life-changing event, he'd found Gallup, New Mexico, to be one of the friendlier cities on Route 66. The people were a mix of Indian, White, and Mexican, so they had learned to tolerate unusual individuals. They were also strong and self-reliant citizens, so a handful of unwashed bikers hadn't been seen as an invading threat to the local culture. *Yep, Gallup is a nice town. Hot, but what burg isn't along this section of Route here in the Southwest?*

Sitting in the back seat of the taxi, watching the dusty landscape drift past, Tim's throat feels more parched than ever. Cumulus clouds are forming a towering line over the ridge of the nearby mountain range. A thunderhead climbs high, its bottom turning blue-black. A dazzling bolt of lightning lashes the brown slope, producing an explosive crack of thunder.

Tim swallows dryly, almost tasting the ozone. *I can get a drink at the casino bar. Maybe even for free.*

He pays the cabbie and hauls his backpack up the wide stairs to the entrance doors of the Burning Rock. Here on a Tuesday morning, July fourteenth, a country-rock band is already blasting out live music. The fun never stops. And the temperature in the casino is kept at a chilling sixty-five degrees designed to make the customers just a bit edgy and quick to get their next bet down.

Security is tight, Tim observes. His bag is inspected and then checked at the valet parking booth. He holds onto his keys, phone, and wallet, but knows that if he hadn't given Boyd the t-shaped section of the Pandora Block, it would surely have been scrutinized with suspicion.

Bypassing a long row of ancient amputee thieves and their flashy electronic cousins, he winds his way beyond the crap tables to the cashier window. The dark-haired

Indian maid behind the gilded cage gives him a smile of brilliant, straight teeth. Her badge identifies her as Crystal.

Tim gives the smile back. "You have an employee here named Nakai? Louis Nakai?"

"Sure do, handsome." She blinks dark eyes, waiting.

"Well, can you get him or tell him I'm here?"

Behind Tim, a slot machine pays out with a whooping series of bing-bong-bings. Otherwise, the casino is relatively quiet, since the band had taken a blessed break. The real crowds and activity will come in the evening, especially during the weekend.

The coy cahier sets her phone receiver back in its cradle. "He'll be right down." The girl flashes her snow whites at him again.

"You didn't give him my name or anything. Very accommodating."

"I didn't have to." She points a turquoise fingernail up at a small video camera mounted on the wall behind her head, just as a woman with an aluminum walker edges up behind Tim and the grilled window.

Tim looks into the lens and runs a forefinger along the side of his nose. It is a gesture from the old days.

"Can we move it along, buster?" The walker woman nudges his elbow with a wrinkled claw.

Tim steps to one side and stands near to a door painted with the earth-tone design of a teepee. There is a peephole at the wigwam's apex.

The old woman rifles through her padded fanny-pack and brings out a folded wad of twenties. Tim turns discreetly away and gets bumped in the butt when the security door swings open.

"Timmy! You are looking fine as frog's hair, you dodger." Louis Nakai has him in a hug before he can step back.

It is a brief embrace, but for Tim, it feels like three sets of tennis. Finally, the Navajo casino employee releases him but rests an affectionate hand on his left forearm.

Tim reaches into his back pocket and extracts a plastic comb, a gesture intended more to break Louis's touch than to adjust his hair. "Good to see you, Featherstone."

"Ah, you remembered my codename." Nakai wears a beaded vest over a black wife-beater shirt printed with the inscription, "The Navajo Knows." His bright eyes gleam apparent joy and, when he tosses his head to one side, short braided pigtails tap his wide cheeks.

Tim figures that this movement is an unconscious habit designed to make Louis seem more attractive. *He's already coming on to me.*

"Step into my laboratory."

They pass through the door and climb a short flight of stairs into a darkened room full of more than a dozen computer screens and video monitors. Louis plops down into a chair on casters and almost spins around, wheels squeaking a little. "I'll call and get you a room at the inn. We have special accommodations for high rollers."

Tim clears his dry throat. "You did get the text I sent you, right?"

"Oh, sure." A small red light begins to blink over the

top of one of the monitors. "Hold on a sec." Louis taps a key on a computer and addresses the air. "Rodney, there's a card-counter at table five. Better move in on him."

Tim is about to ask for a double scotch when an overweight man in his middle-sixties and a loose-fitting suit pushes in. "What's this guy doing up here in the surveillance room?"

Louis comes to his feet, almost at attention. "Relax, boss. He's an old buddy of mine. A reporter from LA here to give us some powerful publicity."

Why not? Tim takes up the tale. "Yeah, I'm working on a feature story for the *Trib* that could help you expand operations into California."

The big man cocks his head. "Yeah? Well, I guess…Nakai, lemme know if you need anything."

Tim tries to act friendly. "I could use a shingled roof."

Louis Nakai snorts at the old joke.

The big guy pauses before leaving, grunting, "The house always wins."

Twenty minutes later, with his shift over, Louis leads the way down past a series of poker tables to a quiet and lavish restaurant. Like all casinos, the entire building is built like a fortress with low lighting and no windows to the outside. Rain rumbles on the roof.

Tim gets his drink as they sit near the far end of a padded bar and watch a sous-chief calmly operate behind the counter. The petit woman grills buffalo steaks on an open flame and skillfully pan-fries shrimp with an assortment of fresh cut veggies. The sizzle and steam surround the two men as they engage in quiet, small talk.

Louis seems edgy. Tim almost spills his drink when the Indian confesses his affection for him. "I think the rain has let up," he responds, hoping to change the subject.

"Then, let's get out of here."

Tim isn't sure what that implies, but he shrugs, collects his bag and follows Louis along a row of tourist buses to where they climb into a late-model Mazda. Nakai drives them through the muggy landscape to the entrance to the reservation. The scene is like something out of an old western, except for the autos parked in front of each small building and the occasional satellite dish.

Parking next to a house that is more of a shack, Tim soon finds himself in a dark living room with windows covered by thick closed curtains. The few chairs are littered with sheets of paper and three-ring binders. The panels from a couple of castoff doors have been laid flat across wooden saw-horses and covered with computer hardware, several laptops, and an impressive printer.

Louis sits down in one of the chairs while making a sweeping gesture with his hands. "From here, I can find anything on the internet, but it's not like the old days."

Tim senses an inner sadness behind his friend's bravado. "Your talents are wasted with all this, Featherstone. Working with Miko, Boyd and me was the best time of your life, remember? We couldn't have succeeded without you."

Louis looks around the dim room and sighs. "I guess

maybe you're right. Sitting in this darkness, I feel older every day."

"Well, you're not exactly a failure, you know.

"You're a natural." Tim rests his rucksack on a sagging couch.

"No, *you're* the natural. You have a fine future as a reporter. I've read your stories in the press, exposing corruption in high places. I'm only one of a million computer geeks marginalized by my race and sexual preference."

"Bull shit! You're a genius. But you're wrong if you think that *I'm* a success. You can still prove yourself and maybe help save the world, at the same time."

"Tell that to the wife who left me or my brother who is making a career for himself in the military."

This guy gets more depressing by the minute. Tim struggles to change the subject. "The disease is the worst thing happening in the world right now."

"I know. We had three black women serving drinks at the casino two months ago. Now they're all gone." Louis wipes an eye. "One, Sandra, was expecting a baby next March. She aborted in order to stay alive."

Tim shudders. "We have a possible cure. That's why I'm here."

"What do you mean?"

"Do you remember that bronze block we all split up when we all—split up?"

"The one with something like 'Pandora' written on it? Boyd gave each of us a section when the team separated."

"I've seen Boyd."

Nakai's attitude perks. "No way," he protests. "He's in prison somewhere in Turkey. It was *your* testimony that put him there."

"Yeah, well…there's a theory that the Block, when assembled, contains a description for a cure to the virus."

Louis laughs. "Are aliens involved, as well?"

"I'm serious. I came here to retrieve your piece."

"I don't have it, Timmy. I lost it two years ago during an insertion into the back country of Colombia."

"A what now?'

"It was my final military op for the army. We were under cover, and I probably shouldn't even be telling you this, but I had it with me when the bulk of my personal possessions were confiscated. We were temporarily captured by the rebels."

This I never knew. "You were in the military?"

"It was my brother's doing. But I was not in for very long. Another of my grand failures."

"Yeah, well, speaking of failures, you might as well know the truth about my current status. I've been fired from my job as an investigative reporter."

"You?"

He hesitates to mention that he'd also been rejected by the woman he adores. "And I've had a rough time recently with Miko Wade, too." *Rough time, indeed.* "She and I are working with Boyd to get the Block assembled." He can't help picturing her in his mind. "She was wearing those cute little earrings I gave her that loop under her lobes."

"Yeah," the Navajo grins. "I've been thinking of getting a pair of—wait. What is all that you just said again about the virus?"

Tim settles onto the couch next to his bag and rubs the back of his neck. "It's perhaps the most important story today. With the Block, we have a chance to find a cure, and you're part of it."

"But I told you I don't have my section any longer. It's gone somewhere in Latin America."

"I get that, but with all your computer skills, do you think there's a chance you could find it?"

Louis smiles. "You know me, Timmy. I'd do just about anything you'd ask."

"In that case, pour me a scotch, and I'll fill you in on the whole story. We've got to find it."

CHAPTER 10

Versailles, France:

Feeling satisfyingly chic and glamorous, Sandrine Lecombe wears a charcoal lace-and-beadwork cardigan with palazzo pants pleated in the front and a black, knee-length imitation fur coat. "I told you over the phone the other day that I'm not interested. Why did you drop by to see me?"

Miko considers her answer. *You have no idea, you clothes horse.* The two women haven't exchanged the customary cheek kisses. Instead, they confront each other, just like old times. "I came from Boyd's villa in the Caribbean. The islands are practically under siege from pirates and low-lives desperate to escape the virus."

"Well, you can go right back then. Things aren't any better in the Hexagon, either." Sandrine toys with her empty wine glass. "Last night, three *arroundissements* went up in massive fires. The palace and park here are all but shut down since the local *banlieues* anticipated a possible riot."

They are meeting inside a wing of the famous chateau of the Sun God. As a curator of the museum, Sandrine maintains a small office on site. It is after hours and, like many of the Paris attractions, the grounds are bereft of the normal visitors and tour-bus caravans.

"Yes, I've heard many of the speculations circulating in the electronic press about of a New Revolution." Miko picks up a glass globe paperweight and studies its flawless interior. "That's why I'm here. I want you to know that we have an outside chance of ending the chaos and possibly curing the Black Sea Virus." She looks up into the other woman's unnaturally colored gray-green eyes. "Interested?"

"That's insane." Sandrine barks a laugh. "How can you and the rest of a bunch of crooks hope or expect to save the world from the worst disease since the Black Death?" She turns and passes through the doorway to walk down the Hall of Mirrors.

Miko puts down the glass globe and follows, not sure where they are going, but having no other choice in the matter. *She's trying to impress me with her position of authority here at the Palace. Childish as ever.*

After about thirty feet of gold and silver reflections, even in the evening's subdued light, they turn right into dual, high-ceilinged chambers filled with ornate furniture from the seventeenth century now stacked together as if awaiting an auction.

They stand together casually and gaze out a long row of ceiling-to-floor windows that face the wide stone terrace. The fountains and gardens stretch silently northwest for almost a mile. Miko wishes she could take Sandrine Lecombe by her elegant long neck and shake some urgency into her. *Off with her head.*

Instead, slowly, carefully, she begins to relate Boyd's story of the inscription on the Pandora Block and how it could quite possibly save humanity from the BSV.

Sandrine relaxes on a chaise lounge beyond the velvet ropes, smoking a Gauloises and letting the ashes flick to the marble floor. Perhaps the world *was* coming to an end if *objets d'art* and national treasures could be so easily and completely disrespected.

"Okay, I've heard your fantastic story, and made my decision." Sandrine crushes out the butt on the soul of her shoe. "I'll give you my piece of the puzzle—if you'll help me get what I want."

"That depends. What do you want?"

Sandrine sits upright, resting her thin hands on her knees and offering a calculated smile. "I want your help acquiring an item from the Louvre."

Miko puffs out some air. "So, even though you're now an art critic and curator, you haven't lost your interest in high-class theft."

Sandrine accepts the cut casually. "I have to keep my hand in if I'm planning to succeed. Like I told you, I'm not interested in saving the world. I just want to get a nice piece of it for myself."

Miko returns the smile, looking directly at the other

woman. "All right. Depending on what the item is. I'm afraid I'm not strong enough to steal 'The Winged Victory' or 'Venus d'Milo.' Much too heavy."

There's that barking laugh again. "How about Leonardo's illustration of Lisa del Giocondo?"

"De Vinci's 'Mona Lisa'? You're kidding, of course. No other treasure, except maybe the Hope Diamond, is more professionally and thoroughly protected."

"Ah," Sandrine waggles a long finger. "You're forgetting the Crown Jewels."

This was crazy. But Miko's whole life has been one crazy thing after another. Still, she dislikes being manipulated, especially by Lacombe. With patience, however, she might be able to get what she came after. "Fine. But you and I know that we scoped that painting out years ago and found its security to be multi-leveled to the point of ridiculousness. The French don't *ever* want to find it stolen again."

"Speaking for the French," Sandrine uses a palm to smooth a lock of her red hair back along the side of her head, "we have a lot more important issues these days than protecting an old but beautiful painting."

"Oh, I forgot. You consider yourself an heir of the dauphine."

Sandrine gives a slight curtsey in acknowledgement of the assumed honor. "I *am* an heir. And it's not the Louvre painting that we're after. It's the detailed sketch made in 1504, still maintained in the museum's sub-basement vault."

"Interesting."

"I thought you'd like it. Some say that it was composed by Raphael due to the detailed flanking columns, background landscape and the youthful demeanor of the model, but I know better."

"Of course you do," says Miko. "And the security?"

"Only an ancient safe. And I have a way to get the combination."

Of course, she did. "Then why do you need me?"

Sandrine Lecombe spreads her arms wide. "I hate to work alone. Besides, the trick isn't getting the original sketch. It's getting it out of the Louvre. I want you to be a distraction."

Miko considers. *So, I'm to be a criminal again. I came here intending to do something worthwhile, and this scheming bitch who never stopped being a thief wants to drag me back into the profession.* "Why do you want the De Vinci sketch?"

"I have a buyer, of course. Someone you might know. Intimately."

"Birol? Is that it? You want to get in good with Birol and try to ease me out?"

Sandrine gives a gleeful squeal that reminds Miko of a wet cat. "Do you want my section of the block, or not, Ms. Wade?"

Even though she has been planning to leave Birol, Miko doesn't like the idea that she might be replaced by this heartless French twist. On the other hand, dealing with Sandrine had never been a problem before and for sure wouldn't matter much now. Miko is certain she can handle the woman's intentions if she remains careful and alert. "All right. I accept and assume that I'll get the piece as soon as you get the sketch. When do we start?"

Lecombe turns to exit the ornate chamber. "Right now. We should have good cover, this being Bastille Day. Paris will be wild."

⌘

Busan, South Korea:

The heart has gone out of these people. Ill health is the principal expression on their faces. Yet the unruly crowd is a race of animals uniquely able to oppose their thumbs to the four other digits and skilled by tradition to burn or inter their dead. With hope, they might survive.

Boyd awakes when the plane lands at the Gimhae airport, west of the city proper. Rubbing his arthritic shoulder, he gathers his things and walks gingerly into the terminal.

A great many law enforcement agents would be surprised to find Jonathan Boyd passing beneath the airport security cameras. These same international police once thought him the most audacious bandit of the twenty-first century.

However, nothing comes of it here and now, just as he's planned, partly due to simple changes in makeup and the more pressing chaotic conditions currently threatening the world.

Clearing customs, he relies on one of his old and trusted comrades for ground transportation. Jae Kim flashes the headlights of a late-model Kia in the driving rain to attract his attention.

Boyd slides his lean form in beside the Korean, tossing his carry-on into the back seat. "Good to see you again, Brother Kim. How's the family?"

Jae grunts, navigating the heavy traffic that streams along Busan's highway. The car crosses the Nakdongdaegyo Bridge for a short ride into town.

"It could have been under better circumstances and conditions. Yes?" Jae Kim, always a natty dresser, is attired in tan slacks, a dark blue sports coat, and a saffron-colored turtleneck shirt. "I had to shake at least one tail before picking you up."

Relaxing and lighting a cigarette with a gold lighter that he'd acquired somewhere in transit from the Caribbean, Boyd utters a faint chuckle. "Always the pessimist, Jae. So what do you make of all this craziness?"

The man behind the wheel presses a button to roll down the passenger-side window and cause a draft that vacuums the smoke from the speed vehicle and into the moist night. "Those things will kill you."

"You could say that about so many things these days," Boyd replies, but he takes the other's meaning and tosses the butt out through the light rain, pressing his own button to ease the window shut.

The car's wiper blades beat a pulsing rhythm as the two "business men" drive through town to the docks. Rows of giant mechanical cranes reach up and out into the gun-metal gray sky.

"Let's deal with what we know, for starters," Jae

Kim replies, steering into a parking space next to a two-story wooden warehouse. "The threat of war from the country up north is growing."

Boyd arches an eyebrow. "Any impending military attack is out of our hands, so let's focus on the root cause of the crisis. That will be dangerous enough."

"You mean the virus." It was not a question. "You forget that I'm a doctor."

"Yes. What has your research discovered? Something that will give us hope?"

"Come inside first and let me check your vitals."

They exit the Kia, ducking and dashing through a sudden ninety-degree -angle shower.

CHAPTER 11

I see that you're favoring your right shoulder. Let me take a look at it."

"It's just a touch of arthritis from the dank prison," says Boyd.

"Still the dashing rouge, eh? Take your shirt off."

Boyd unbuttons his cuffs and shirt front. He shrugs his shoulders, exposing the mass of scar tissue on his back and upper chest.

Jae Kim can't help taking a step back upon seeing the cicatrix map on the tall man's body. "Some of these look like acid burns."

Boyd sighs. "Imagine that."

Jae Kim unscrews the lid from a jar of pearl-hued cream and applies the salve to Boyd's right deltoid. The lights flicker momentarily before coming back on dimmer than before.

"This is what I think of when I imagine how life

must have been like during your famous Dark Ages." Jae Kim expertly works the cream into Boyd's tender joint and muscles. "The electrical grid comes and goes, disrupting communication and transportation throughout the city. Water shortages are beginning. Fresh vegetables have doubled in price in the last few weeks."

Boyd feels the other man's expert ministrations and understands his need to vent. The storm is still blowing outside the building.

"News comes from all directions, but it contradicts itself until you don't know what to believe, even about the weather forecast." The Korean continues to knead the area, warming it as the pain lessened. "Clinics and ERs are overwhelmed with patients imagining that their slightest sneeze or cough means death. The IMF is warning that the US will soon default on its loans, rendering the country's treasury bills worthless. I haven't had a good cup of coffee in over a month."

"You're ranting, Jae."

"Am I? Am I really?" Kim comes around and looks directly into Boyd's eyes. "Let me tell you what I know of the BSV. It begins by breaking down the inter-uterine wall, destroying the tissue until an unborn child cannot come to term. Then the woman becomes painfully sterile, especially if she's a Black woman."

To Boyd, it is a terrifying thought. *A deadly condition like sickle cell anemia that targets a specific race.* Only this disease is bloody and painful, as well as being fatal.

"The human papillomavirus is biologically compelled to reproduce itself as often as possible," Jae continues, "as if it were programmed to attack the DNA of a specific part of mankind. Fortunately, it has yet to go airborne or mutate to affect the Asian races or the Caucasians. I've been trying to develop a vaccine—"

"And how's that going?" Boyd interrupts, pulling his shirt back on.

Jae Kim turns to the sink, scrubbing the last of the cream from his fingers. "It's not. The CDC found a genetic 'cousin' of the virus and began inoculations, but it appears that the cure does not work on the vast majority of the infected population, especially those living in the northern regions of Africa. It's almost as if it had been manufactured to destroy the Black race."

"No," Boyd counsels. "It's naturally occurring."

"How do you know?"

Instead of answering, the elder man poses his own question. "What if I were to tell you that I have a lead on a possible cure?" Quickly, carefully, Boyd lays out the information gleaned from Kultar regarding the Pandora Block. As he does so, he stands and stretches. The shoulder feels remarkably pain free now. *Warm, too.*

Jae Kim listens, skeptical at first, but then his brow tightens as he considered Boyd's tale. "Vector analysis of the earliest reported cases points to the northern coast of Turkey, near the city of Terme. But some cases were also reported along the northeastern coast of the Black Sea."

"Thus, the virus's name," Boyd agrees. The lights flickered again.

A young Asian girl opens the door without knocking

and enters the room, as if she owns it. She announces something in Korean before stopping to stare with Capri-blue eyes.

Jae Kim answers her curtly and turns to Boyd. "This is my little sister, Gi-cho. She says that dinner will be ready in five minutes."

The girl smiles. "Oh, sorry. English?" She is cute, in a waifish way, about five feet tall and petite all over, with short tousled hair and intent eyes. "Jonathan Boyd. A pleasure to meet you."

He bows slightly. *Seems appropriate.*

During a meal of fish pancakes, the two men discuss the importance of the Block and its inscription. Gi-cho hovers near, attending to the conversation and arranging plates of steaming food. Almost too near, thinks Boyd.

Jae Kim cradles a porcelain bowl in both hands and sipped pale tea from it. "Unfortunately, the section of the bronze cube that you gave me was stolen by a few months back by a lab assistant. She had volunteered to work here for almost no pay. I later found out that it was in order to gain access to drugs and medical equipment. I should have known better than to employ a member of an urban street gang."

"Then we must find her," Gi-cho puts in.

The two men stare at each other. Jae Kim seems about to remonstrate, when Boyd asserts, "She's right. Have you any idea where your ex-assistant can be located?"

Jae Kim frowns, but the girl's small smile widens.

❧❧

Paris, France:

Miko Wade steps out from the Metro car at the Rue de Rivoli station and meets Sandrine near the entrance to the Musee du Louvre. Due to the Bastille Day celebration, the rail line is in operation past two a.m., but few passengers exit here this late at night, since the main *fete nationale* is still taking place above ground where fireworks continue to illuminate the night sky.

An hour earlier in her hotel suite, Miko had not been able to find her false eyelashes, nor her spare set. *Dumb, dumb, dumb.* Then, she'd realized that somehow her room had been broken into and searched. There were more serious things to worry about than her makeup. As a result, she'd made a few calls and brought along a couple electronic items that had been delivered by Birol's security team.

Sandrine Lecombe is not going to get the best of me, she vows, as the two women move past the pale bust of Socrates and the weathered Egyptian statues on display in the Metro station that is connected to the museum.

Miko notes that, like she, Sandrine has dressed as inconspicuously as possible in flats, a dark pantsuit despite the warm night and hair tied back out of the way of any sudden movements.

The art critic has discarded her jewelry, but Miko wears the green and cream cameo necklace given to her months before when Birol had been feeling ultra-cautious and frisky.

Why are we entering from this direction? Miko's

nerves are becoming raw. She needs to get herself on solid ground.

She had worked tangentially with Sandrine on a couple of Boyd's minor projects years ago—a handoff from picking a diplomate's pocket and a getaway after a rare coin theft from a low-level Russian official. The two women had been an essential part of the clandestine break-in almost six years earlier at Birol's Turkish estate. Together, with the other five members of the team, they had made off with nearly two-hundred million dollars of priceless, timeless art objects, including a dozen Fabergé Eggs and the singular Pandora Block.

Now, ducking her head from security cameras as she entered the expansive alcove beneath the Louvre's glass pyramid, Miko catches sight of a whimsical man in a tweed suit, sporting a pair of lime-green glasses on his thin, pointed nose.

Good God! What has she gotten herself into? Miko takes in a startled breath and brings up the single-reflex lens camera she totes on one shoulder—an innocent-looking but deadly device that can crack a skull when swung by her expert hands.

"Wait. Stop," Sandrine whispers harshly. The woman raises a forearm to block Miko's intended blow. "He's on our side. Gerard, this is the woman I spoke to you about."

Miko manages a smile, steeling herself.

The short man rises out of a half crouch, tucks an umbrella under his arm and extends a hand in welcome, although Miko can still see fear and a touch of cunning in his coffee-colored eyes as he answers, "*Enchante.*"

Miko casts a glance at Sandrine. "Museum employ-ee?"

The smile on the other woman's red lips widens. "Curator and inside man."

Gerard places an index finger beside his nose. "I'm honored to meet the famous—"

Both women cut off his words before he could utter a formal name.

Distant fireworks from the direction of the Eiffel Tower blossom in the sky and are captured in the steel and glass net of the pyramid overhead.

"We need to hurry this along," says Miko. *I don't like surprises, and I definitely don't like being out-numbered.*

Sandrine nods, seeming to agree. "Come." She pats a thin attaché case that Gerard carries. "We only have a short time before the effects of the EMwave generator wears off against the palm readers, bio scans, and digital camera systems."

The three thieves move down a darkened passage and descend into the museum's lower Sully level. They wind their way single-file around the curved wall of the medieval moat. The pale yellow arched stone walls da-ting back to the twelfth century when the original struc-ture had been part of a fortress stood strong and mute. The interlopers creep forward to access a pair of metal doors labeled in three languages, indicating *CLOSED*.

Miko wonders how they are going to proceed, since all the electrical security systems supposedly have been stunned by Gerard's EMwave device. But the little man is un-daunted. From the inside pocket of his suit coat, he produces a five-inch, tarnished key that would likely open the portal of any fairy tale castle.

God bless the nostalgic, romantic French. Miko hears something click in the door's lock. It reminds her of the inner workings of an ancient clock. The right-hand door eases open silently, as if on oiled hinges.

Sandrine gestures for Miko to enter. "Now, the fun begins."

CHAPTER 12

Sandrine illuminates the gloom with a tiny flame from her lighter. All around are horizontal file cabinets, shelves of drawers, and racks of paintings stacked individually flat in protected plastic sheets. In the dimness, Miko can see packing cases and crates—some half open, others sealed with ancient wax.

Gerard, being a curator, appears to know exactly where he is headed. Without hesitation, he draws open a drawer from one of the metal cabinets and extracts a small framed picture.

Leaning over the man's shoulder, Miko studies the sketch executed on finely woven cloth, almost like silk. *Did they have silk in the sixteenth century Europe?* The texture of the sketch's surface seems layered with a thin film that gave back a glossy glow in the subdued light.

The fabric has been mounted and stretched on a plain wooden frame darkened with age. Sandrine works quickly to cut the sketch from the heavy staples that held it in place on the wood.

Snick. Snick

Uncomfortably impatient, Miko longs to scratch an itch beneath her left bra strap. She realizes she'd been holding her breath. Letting it out now, she adjusts for the low lighting and snaps a series of photos with the camera fastened to the sturdy black band around her neck.

The sketch itself measures sixteen inches square on the tanned cloth. Once, it might have been created by a crude sort of waxed crayon. Now centuries later, the image of the coy woman's head, shoulders, and crossed hands seemed indelibly imprinted into the fabric.

Gerard carefully rolls the smooth cloth into a cylindrical shape with a diameter no larger than half an inch. Then he inserts the fabric tube into the folds of the black umbrella he's been carrying. He securely snapped the folds shut and tucks the dark parasol under his left arm, smiling like a contented cat.

But even though his electronic device has fouled the electronic surveillance systems, there is one security program still in operation. A beam from a high-intensity flashlight flares from behind the trio. The stern voice of a night watchman commanded, *"Haut la mains!"*

The order only served to propel the thieves forward. Sandrine tosses her lighter aside, setting fire to a bundle of excelsior which quickly spreads to a draped curtain. With a banshee shriek, she grabs the pole attached to the flaming curtain and flourishes it at the startled guard's head.

Without conscious thought, Miko dashes past the man and back into the main gallery, accompanied by the Gerard and Sandrine. They leave the guard to stamp out the fire and run down a corridor and up a flight of wide stairs.

Miko knows that other guards will quickly respond to the commotion and give chase. In a matter of seconds, she and her companions scurry through a series of rooms that showcase Italian paintings. Titian, Raphael, Caravaggio—all go by in a blur of muted colors and shadows. Finally, they reach the large, open chamber where the Mona Lisa, itself, had once been displayed before museum officials had moved the painting to a more secure location.

Sandrine calls out something unintelligible, leading the way down a series of marble steps to a single-door exit on the Ponte des Lions. This little-known access to the museum takes the three thieves out to the night traffic on the Quai Francois Mitterrand.

The side of a speeding delivery truck clips Gerard, slamming the little man into Miko and sending him toward the stone embankment above the river. The camera around her neck arcs out and snaps back on its strap, striking her forehead like a steel projectile propelled by a medieval sling.

Miko sees a flare of explosive brilliance accompanied by a sharp pain that penetrates through the back of her head. She stumbles, thrusting out a hand to steady herself, and spies Gerard teetering on the top of the concrete embankment.

Guards, with truncheons raised and waving, pour out of the museum, dodging to either side of the offending truck which speeds into the night. A black BMW parked farther down the street blinks all its lights and blares its horn repeatedly. Sandrine has preset the vehicle as a distraction should they need it to confuse or distract any pursuit. The plan works now as the guards are attracted to the siren call of the high-pitched wail and blazing lights.

Through a haze of pain and disorientation, Miko reaches out to grasp at Gerard's body as it slipped over the wall. *I can only grasp hold of the umbrella.* She struggles to pull him to safety. But Gerard's hand slides inexorably down the length of the slick, black cloth. The man with the green glasses tilts and falls head first down toward the Quai des Tuileries below. There is the sudden sound of a splat from below beside the concrete bank of the silent Seine. His stunned expression is a mask of gray and scarlet.

Still holding the umbrella and its precious contents, Miko feels herself thrust by Sandrine in the direction of another, smaller car. The two women tumble into a Deux Chevaux Citroen, while the guards continue to collect around the blaring BMW farther down the street.

Sandrine kicks the starter, shifting the little buzzing car into gear, and the two women speed up the quai into the darkness, just as the first police van screeches to a halt at the other end of the street.

Miko's senses clear enough for her to understand Sandrine's insistent query: "Have you got it?"

A gasp, and then an unsteady, "Yes."

"Sweet."

"Where are we going?"

"To my place, dear, where we can make the exchange."

సౌసౌ

Busan, South Korea:

Jae Kim is relieved to find that there are few passengers in the subway car that carry Boyd, Gi-cho, and himself toward the Haedong Yongkungsa temple remains. At this early hour, corporation and factory workers are too busy rushing to their places of employment. They cough and show no interest in stopping at a once-popular tourist site.

Jae cannot believe that society has come so close to death. *This must be what life was like during the time of the Black Plague. Thousands die daily because help cannot arrive in time.*

He glances at his sister seated next to Boyd. Families like mine are splitting apart, he realizes. Minor disagreements have grown into fierce disputes as relatives fight for what they believe to be the best way to survive. The doomsday clock is only seconds away from midnight. By now, millions must be infected, and countries like North Korea are desperately plotting nuclear sanitation of what they consider highly-infected populations. *We could all die at any second, and there is no protection—yet.*

The subway car streams along its tracks, rising above

ground and briefly encountering the early morning light. Gi-cho stands up carefully within the speeding public transportation car and comes to sit beside him. She dips her head, cleared her throat and asks if Boyd is truly a thief.

Jae Kim scans the features of his friend, the man across the aisle. Eyes sharp, chin erect, Boyd seems intent on studying the shoreline northwest of the city as it rushed past.

"He is a very good thief," Kim answers in a hushed tone, envisioning the scars he'd treated beneath the older man's shirt. "He has stolen many rare and well-guarded items during his long career. And he is principled, having perfected the small aspects of his life to a point where he accepts responsibility for sharing the spoils of his skills."

A small indent appears on Gi-cho's smooth brow, but she does not pose a question, only a look from one man to the other.

The train rattles on. So does Jae Kim. "His thinking is that he actually gets more by giving. His status as a thief results from the general welfare that comes from his expertise for acquiring things that are hidden."

"Complex," his sister remarked, "and romantic."

Jae Kim frowns for a second. "What are you thinking, mouse?"

"In another life, he could have been an archeologist. But that would have been too dull and dirty for him."

"More likely, he would have been a top analyst for his Central Intelligence Agency or the British MI-Six."

"No," the girl sighs. "That again would be too dull and slightly dirty."

Boyd shifts position in his seat next to the window. Kim wonders if the man overheard part of the conversation. If so, he gives no sign.

Gi-cho whispers, nearly in awe. "A man of mystery."

Jae Kim pinches the bridge of his nose with his fingertips, exhales and shakes his head.

ͽͼ

Calcutta, India:

The latest reports did not look good. It is the fifth month of major loses.

Birol calls his Chief Financial Officer into the office decorated with Grecian mosaics from Antioch and first-century friezes. One wall is completely covered by a fragment of an Egyptian stone relief framing the goddess Hathor granting protection to Seti I.

"As I explained before, Mr. K," the tall, lean man's voice rolls out as smooth as honey to his employer, "these are minor adjustments to your accounts that will be reallocated once appropriate, high-gain investments have been located."

Birol toys with the expresso cup before him on his Japanese-lacquer and gilded-bronze desk, circa 1780. He struggles to overcome a strong urge to fling it in the face of his overpaid accountant. "Only a fool would think I'd believe there were high-gain investments still available in a world rapidly going to hell." His voice is flat. "Where is this money? My money?"

The thin CFO blanches. He taps the smartwatch next to the virgin white shirt cuff on his left wrist. "That would be," he says stiffly, "in a Cayman account, where we—"

Birol rises to his full height, still a foot shorter than his associate. "I personally closed that account at the CNB two days ago."

The executive swallows. He starts to explain further, piling a new lie on top of the old, but Birol again cuts him off. "Consider yourself fired." The billionaire lets his distended dark eyes penetrate into the other man's expression, possibly his soul. "And so is your brother, even though he recently informed me of your betrayal of my trust."

"Sir, Mr. K, if I may—"

"I hate thieves!"

"But, sir—"

"I have your wife, as well as your daughter. They will be returned as soon as my money is."

The man is shaken and begins to pale. His shoulders slump, and he seems to shrink.

Birol gives him an impatient wave of the hand. "You have until this time tomorrow. Make good use of it."

Yes, sir," the ex-executive replies in an even voice which makes Birol all the more suspicious.

"And if you attempt to flee, abandoning your family, I'll have you completely terminated."

                                      John Hegenberger

"Yes, sir." The man's tone is much more uneven this time. He slowly turns to leave the room.

Birol smiles.

ↂↄↂↄ

Everywhere:

The inorganic reaches out to further invade the organic. A thick membrane protects the inner elements. Chemical nerves latch onto rich biomass. Wet sacks of genetic material vibrate and pulsed to a slow inner rhythm. Captured biomass converts to a new generation of viral segments easily assembled. Mutating poison into hosts blocking biological attacks. Dictating death. Mindlessly implanting. Pulsing. Implanting. Pulsing. Implanting. Bursting. Implanting.

CHAPTER 13

Calcutta, India:

Boyd shifts in his seat to get a better look at the low buildings and thick foliage that flashed past the window in the dawning light. He reflects on the snatches of the conversation he's picked up as the train car hums through the Land of the Morning Calm.

In its purest form, the life of a thief is one filled with risk, stealth, and exhilarating gain. Despite the sea of social media that Boyd is only just now learning about since his incarceration, so much in today's world is still locked away, hidden from the general population. In many respects, it always has been. Secret truths, off-the-record bank accounts, valuable artifacts all are sealed away where few individuals have access, and, thus, the day-to-day reality settles into a soft-edge white lie.

Boyd's career in this gray, shadowy world began

when he learned the story of his family's role in hiding the truth. At first, he wanted to share what he'd discovered, but soon he realized that almost no one would believe or accept it. Instead, he took to searching for and collecting similar, highly-classified facts, finding patterns and links that connected the lies and omissions. Gradually, all this secret information combined into a reality that most people wouldn't believe to be the truth—but is.

Along the way, he encountered other treasures—passcodes, encrypted data that opened fat bank accounts and safety deposit boxes stuffed with jewels and foreign currency. The vast wealth of a cloistered world easily tumbled into his hands. His skills for illicit discovery became more and more well-honed.

Within a few short years, he had amassed his own treasure trove not just of financial value, but of hidden knowledge, until one day he knew he had a choice. He could either hide away his own loot like those before him or he could break the mold of the standard thief and let it all go back where it could do the most good. The knowledge, he could secretly share, like Snowden had, releasing it discreetly to the press, exposing the clandestine operations of governments, agencies, and institutions. The physical items of worldly value—jewels, art objects, and paintings, could be turned to cash or donated anonymously to public museums and organizations of higher learning.

It was itself a tricky operation, at first, yet gradually Boyd succeeded in creating a sort of machine that took the raw material of hidden riches and converted it to finished goods given to institutions dedicated to sharing the wealth of human experience.

There was a grand satisfaction in all that. Part of this machine was the careful assemblage of his acquisitions team—men and women skilled at locating that which others had locked away. Some members of the team, like Louis Nakai, were professionals at data-mining and analysis. Others, like Tim Cross and dear Miko Wade, were able to read people and situations to seek out the latent truth. Still others like Sandrine Lecombe and Hank Jones, where naturally intuitive in strategy and tactics. They could penetrate to the core of a circumstance and move directly with the least number of steps or hindrance to proficiently achieve the goal.

Together, under Boyd's direction, the team had performed a number of successful heists, years ago, unknown to the public. Nazi treasure holds still hidden in Argentina, Alexandrian library artifacts and Solomon troves buried in distant Egyptian sands. Bank accounts of world leaders, politicians, and high-level executives—all were carefully uncovered and secretly distributed to the delight and amazement of the common man, who never knew or suspected that Boyd's acquisitions team operated or even existed.

The cool irony of thieves stealing from thieves on such a grand scale was exhilarating. It had made Boyd feel whole, complete, justified and electrically alive. But, it never occurred to him that one member of his team might think it all unjustified. The Judas had been Tim Cross.

A sharp whistle sounds. The string of railcars begins to slow. In the distant, beyond the train's smoke-glass window, the vertical mountains and ridges of the countryside hide Seoul, the capital of South Korea, as well as its northern "neighbor" and the danger beyond the DMZ where Communists have massed along the border for decades. *Some things never seem to change.*

"This is our stop." Gi-cho rises and indicates a pale-blue sign at the station. Haedong Yonggungsa. "The temple is a small distance farther up the shore."

Just as they exit the station on foot, the storm intensifies again. Sudden sheets of drilling rain lance down from the dark clouds that have rolled overhead like a thousand smoke bombs. Within seconds, Boyd and the others of his small party are soaked and scrambling into the entrance pavilions and the steep stairs that lead down to the temple.

The walls of the passageway are pitted with age. Rivulets of rainwater overflow the bamboo gardens on either side of the concrete path and stream from dark crevices between the ancient stones.

Gi-cho wrings water from her hair with both hands and leads the way farther down the stairs past a long row of stone lanterns and statues of erect dogs guarding the entrance. Boyd catches a brief glimpse of the roiling gray sea through a stand of pine trees as they neared the rocky shore. Foaming waves thrust up and under a white bridge.

Jae Kim leans into the driving rain. "The things I do to find a cure." He splashes through a deep puddle, nearly slipping.

They enter a low-ceilinged chamber where sit three squat Buddha statues covered with flaking gold paint. An intricate flower décor covers a teak railing and a wooden dais. Obscure glyphs have been carved long ago into the stone walls.

Boyd says nothing but keeps a sharp eye for any movement among the shadows out beyond a similar lonely Buddha statue on the spindrift-swept cliff thirty feet away.

But the sudden confrontation comes from a direction none of them expected. A handful of the shabby faithful has followed them silently down the stairs to pay their respects, seeking blessings. Now, these people prove to be no ordinary followers. Four of the six figures step up from behind carrying knives at their sides. One, a trim woman, holds a length of pipe, resting it casually on her right shoulder, like a Louisville slugger. In the pounding rain, all are dripping and intent on confronting Boyd and his friends. The words, "street gang," flashed through his mind. *We're in for a robbery.*

Gi-cho takes a step toward the gang of six. Jae Kim reaches out an arm to stop her, but is too slow. His sister places her palms together under her chin and bows slightly at the waist. Immediately, the gang spreads out, each member distancing itself from the others to form a human semi-circle or half noose around Gi-cho and her two companions.

The girl with the ugly pipe has let much of her dark, wet hair hang over her eyes, as if affecting an inky disguise.

But Kim seems to recognize her during a brilliant flash of lightning. He steps around his sister to stand face-to-face with the threatening woman.

A sudden crack of thunder sends a shiver down Boyd's spine. *Or is it only a trickle of cold rain water?* He keeps his feet planted apart and his hands open for all to see.

A man with high cheek bones and scruffy dark facial hair moves forward, challengingly.

Jae Kim calls to the woman, who now cradles the pipe in her left palm. "Eun Kwan Choi. I see you've fallen back into your old way of life."

The woman smiles. "Doctor Kim. You have no idea."

The scruffy-bearded Nam Joon interrupts, adopting English to clearly communicate his intent. "I am Nam Joon Hyun, and you North Korean spies are our captives."

"Now wait," Boyd cautions awkwardly through the heavy downpour.

"We know how to deal with agents of the North when they attempt to infiltrate our installation."

Boyd mumbles to himself, "Infiltrate?"

The girl with the pipe speaks up again. "The little sister has nothing to do with this, I'm certain. She should be taken back up the hill to the temple entrance. She is dumber than soup."

"No," says Gi-cho, already struggling with one of the street gang.

Kim is quick to counter. "You are right, Eun Kwan.

She shouldn't even be here. She followed me out of foolishness."

The scruffy leader gives a gesture to have Kim's sister taken around a water fountain shaped like a turtle and back up the stairs. Then, Boyd finds himself quickly frisked and led through the driving rain, past the golden Buddha statue at the edge of the cliff. *I should have thought it through better. Or at least brought a weapon.*

A hatch behind the statue is yanked open, and the two men are taken down, below sea level to an old bunker, probably built originally by the US military fifty years ago.

Boyd struggles against a wave of panic brought on by the vivid memory of his years in prison. "A street gang possessing an abandoned shore battery," he says to no one in particular.

Once again, he realizes how the world he has known has been pushed aside, first by the virus, and then by the after-effects of fear. Life has become a series of challenges, and everyone is now justifiably out for their own gain.

"Opportunities arise for the industrious and the clever," replies the gang leader with contempt.

Boyd adopts a casual stance. "And the careful, I should think."

Nam Joon shoots him a glance, while bragging. "We are extremely careful."

As the storm outside continues to build, the two men are ushered into a cramped control room where the questioning began.

Jae Kim insists that they are only there to retrieve the

BP section from Eun Kwan. She has placed it among the junk in a desk drawer near a missile-control station.

Boyd notes the painted-over radiation symbol on a cracked wall already oozing sea water.

Kim mumbles something to him about how the missiles might still be armed.

Nam Joon overhears this and comes forward, boldly. "So I was correct. You *are* here as agents of the North Koreans." He instructs his gang, "Lock them in the empty munitions vault. They have value as hostages for ransom."

Three of the followers move in, grasping at their captives. Jae Kim tries to shrug one man off, while Boyd, the tallest person in the room, turns to confront the two other knife welders. He twists to one side, evading a poorly-thrust blade as Kim kicks out, slamming a heavy metal table into a row of desks.

Boyd manages to get his jacket partially wrapped around his left forearm as a defense against a lunging knife.

The table and desks impact the seeping wall. The cracks widen, spraying a powerful stream of water across the small room.

Boyd sees an opportunity and grasps the keyboard of an industrial-strength computer. He swings it into the side of an attacker's head, hearing a satisfying crunch as it crushed the man's nose. From the corner of his eye, he sees the girl swing the pipe in an arch intended for his face.

Then, with a chilling roar, the leaking wall breaks

completely open, and the room becomes a maelstrom of gushing sea water.

CHAPTER 14

Bogota, Columbia:

Tim swears that he'll soon drown in his own perspiration. The oppressive humidity when he and Nakai passed through customs and came out of the El Dorado International airport terminal that Thursday afternoon caused the sweat to pour from his forehead, stinging his eyes. "Jesus, it's hot."

"In Latin America," Louis cautions him, "you should not take the Lord's name in vain."

Tim only grunts and slings his backpack into a dilapidated taxi. "That's another thing we disagree on. When it's hot, I say it's hotter than hell."

Louis nods. "That's better." He gives the driver in a thread-bare baseball cap the name of a local hotel and settles back in the seat before adding: "This should be a job for some government agency, not us."

Tim works the stiffness out of his neck. "Yes, but *you* know where to look, and the people here know you, so we can get it faster. Right?" The avenues and lanes outside their non-air-conditioned cab are crowded with citizens and shopkeepers preparing for the country's impending Independence Day celebration. Tim watches two boys in white shirts stare into the lens of a street-vendor's accordion camera. Lizards chase up cypress trunks. Bearded, elderly men sit in white suits on benches in a small park filled with hanging plants

"I suppose," Louis answers. "And it's good to do something—or anything—worthwhile, instead of waiting for the virus to mutate and spillover into another race, like the Asians or the Whites."

"Or the Dine people. Did I pronounce that right?"

"I know what you mean, Timmy, but just say Navajo and you'll be all right."

Earlier in the week, a powerful earthquake had struck this part of Colombia. Its epicenter was ten miles east of the city. The quake triggered floods, and a wall of water had swept through the area. Heavy rains had previously soaked the nearby hills, and a whole mountainside had slid loose, ripping the jungle, snapping bridges, burying villages and highways.

There is rationing and demonstrations in several parts of the city. Soldiers guard grocery stations and filling stations. The sweltering humidity and high elevation of the Colombian town weigh on Tim and Louis, slowly sapping their energy and keeping them to their own hazy thoughts.

Tim Cross has always believed in doing the right thing. *Even if it was at the wrong time.* Yes, his timing was often just a little off. You'd think he would have learned years ago, when he'd unfortunately chosen the wrong time to run away from home. Or when he'd decided to follow in his father's career as a private investigator. Or when he'd set his sights on Miko Wade while supposedly studying criminology at USC. All these past events had seemed right at the time, but later they each burdened him with goodly amounts of loss and failure.

He'd been beaten and robbed when he ran away from the quiet life of Central Ohio. He'd been shammed and bankrupted when he tried to emulate his father's profession in Southern California. And he'd been rejected and slapped when he courted and partnered with the young and witty Miko. All wrong results from trying to do what felt right.

He knew he wasn't the brightest bulb on the marquee, but he continued to apply himself and never gave up. It was important to keep on keeping on because that was how you got things right—eventually, he thought. By trial and error—only for Tim, it was mostly error. But he always kept trying.

When the PI agency had finally gone bust, Tim had followed Miko and gradually became part of Jonathan Boyd's team. Right from the start, he could see that Boyd's idea of seeking and sharing the truth was the right thing to do. Even if it meant bending a few rules or breaking a couple of laws. Tim's investigative skills, learned from his dad, flourished under Boyd's direction and Miko's confident support. At least, at first.

Soon the three of them were finding and exposing corruption at the highest levels of several world governments. The team became relentless in digging deep undercover, penetrating illegal defenses and stealing info and ill-gotten gains from spreadsheets, vaults, and secured databases. Tim loved it, mostly because it was the right stuff for the twenty-first century.

Always a romantic, he'd tumbled into something, at last, that he was good at. And Miko respected him for it, too. It was the best of all worlds. An investigator who made a true difference in the larger picture and impressed the woman he loved.

"Good gravy, I'd forgotten how muggy this place can be during the storm season," Louis declares.

There is only the slightest of breezes, almost as strong as Louis' exaltation. Tim's armpits are sticky, especially during the slow cab ride. He wishes he'd worn shorts, but has heard that there are voracious insects and other critters down in the tropics that will quickly feast on bare calves.

The sun here burns fiercer than anything he's experienced in LA. He finds that his eyes are locked in a constant wince from the glare. He watches out the window of the slow-moving taxi for some place to get a drink. Even a club soda and lime would be quenching. *Scratch that.* He's heard the tales about drinking South American water. It is not something you risk or question.

And, he has never questioned Boyd's direction or his choice of missions, either. During each operation, throughout the years, it had always been clear what the team was to do and why. Except for the one time that involved billionaire Birol Kalic. As always, Tim and the rest of the growing team accepted what Boyd told them when he'd described Birol as a thug who thirsted after the top rung of the world's ladder, regardless of whose fingers he stepped on.

Prior to this, they had succeeded in besting other corporate giants like Birol, so there was no serious questioning the given details. Working in secret, the team had discovered pharmacological cures withheld from the public for the sake of manipulating the market and driving up demand and profits. They had exposed similar operations regarding hidden oil fields in the Bering Strait and caches of artificial diamonds locked away in Zurich bank vaults.

In each previous case, the cause had been just and the rich results exposed. The operation against Birol had seemed the same sort of case, but then Tim saw that Boyd had an ulterior motive and a personal reason for stealing the billionaire's art collection. And Tim did not think that that was right.

Swallowing dryly now, he watches Louis seated beside him in the back of the hot taxi, tapping his fingers and humming some upbeat show-tune under his breath. The people out in the streets don't seem to mind the heat that surrounded them. They all come from generation upon generation that has grown up in this climate. Tim has a hunch that the Santa Ana winds of Southern California would feel to the locals like chilled air from a meat locker. *Funny how your environment changes your perception. Your fears and doubts, too.*

Tim had repeatedly discussed his suspicions about Boyd with Miko. She thought he was paranoid. He'd spent a sleepless night running the situation over and over through his mind from various points of view. No matter how he considered it, it still seemed wrong that Boyd had sent the acquisitions team off to steal Birol's treasured collection.

It was common knowledge that the billionaire had purchased the Pandora object legally and legitimately from the previous owner at the Turkish museum. Birol was known for running a legitimate business and supporting the development of aviation research with his SpaceZ program.

He had funded more charities than all of Boyd's philanthropic operations combined. It almost seemed as if they were going up against a competitor in the business of robbing from the haves and giving to the have-nots.

So, why take away the billionaire's prized possessions, unless out of shear envy? And why, when confronted, had Boyd refused to explain the justification? Something had not seemed right. Something needed to be done to make things right.

Tim had considered several options and finally fell back on the one that was just like Boyd's basic mode of operation—expose the truth and bring the light of public knowledge to the situation. Do the right thing. Only, for Tim, it was again all wrong.

Once exposed, Boyd had been arrested. He'd managed to escape and meet with the team one last time, where the master thief had handed out the sections of Birol's sacred Pandora Block, as if he were dealing cards or distributing communion. The Europol authorities had arrived and taken him into custody.

Tim and Miko had fled, but her feelings for Tim had turned to hate. She swore she never wanted to lay eyes on him again.

Miko had been right. And Tim had been wrong. Stealing from Birol hadn't been nearly important enough to cause the team to break up. The good that they had collectively accomplished ended with Boyd's imprisonment.

Miko had disappeared from his life, and he didn't even try to trace her. He'd taken to drinking too much, capturing himself in the prison of the bottle. He'd stumbled into a job, using his investigative skills, such as they were, to become a third-rate news reporter. But even that now had begun to spiral downward.

More than once, in his drunken haze, he'd dreamt of the days when things had gone right. During those dreams, he'd awaken to the sound of his own voice calling out for Miko.

Sweating now more than ever, Tim fans his face with a folded newspaper. He'd picked it up when they'd climbed out from the back seat of the taxi, hadn't he? *In this heat, it's hard to remember.* The stories in the paper are in Spanish, but the soccer-game photos are universal. Down below the fold, it looks like there is a story about a government raid of a rebel outpost thirty miles southeast in the jungle.

When asked about it, Nakai nods. "That might be the guy we're looking for."

"Small world," Tim comments dryly.

"Copy that. In this country, you could fling a cat and hit an insurrectionist."

"Let's just hit the bar instead and get a drink, eh?"

CHAPTER 15

Busan, South Korea:

Salty sea water gushes over Jae Kim's head, flooding his eyes and filling his mouth as he gasps for a lungful of clear air. The involuntary urge to cough makes his neck muscles want to explode. He holds onto what little breath he still has and kicks off the side of a control console in an effort to rise above the coursing jet of icy ocean that spewed from the breach in the sub-sea wall.

Through blurred vision, he catches sight of the gang leader, Nam Joon's, body floating face down in the swirling torrent. A foot-long jagged chuck of angle iron juts from the left side of his neck.

A thick cloud of reddish haze smears the water around his stricken, stiff face. The inert form drifts past on an unseen current, nudging Jae Kim's right shoulder as he struggles to gain balance on the slanted top of the control station.

One foot slips and he almost plunges back under the rapidly rising waterline.

His immediate concern is for the safety of his sister. But then, he recalls that Gi-cho had been led away aboveground before the chamber began flooding and—

Boyd! Where's Boyd?

Kim shakes the water from his face and sweeps his eyes across the dimly-lighted room. The passage to the stairs is still fully open. The waterline froths higher up the steps, as Kim sputters and calls out Boyd's name.

Dog-paddling, he notices that the room's illumination is coming from below. He ducks his head into the streaming wet surface and sees a wobbling variety of control lights and glowing computer screens. From the shadows beyond the dashboards, a figure like a clothed porpoise rises in Jae Kim's direction.

A head breaks the surface of the cascading liquid and Boyd's gray eyes almost glow with intensity beneath his dripping brows. "You all right?" the elder man asks in a surprisingly calm voice.

"Let's get the hell out of here."

Boyd spits out a mouthful of water before again speaking. "The section of the Block. I think I've found it. Going back down for it."

"This place is filling up like a giant toilet!"

"I'll be quick." Boyd sucks in a deep breath and descends again beneath the churning surface.

Jae Kim shakes his head with regret. "I'll help you,"

he huffs, splashing down after his friend.

A deep gurgling fills his ears. He kicks off and glides across the section of the room, hearing a dull beeping sound as he neared the control panel where Boyd riffles through the scrambled contents of a side drawer. The beeping becomes louder as he nears the man.

A stream of bubbles rolls up in front of Kim's eyes at the moment when Boyd raises a hand that holds a zig-zagged chuck of copper-colored metal. The thief smiles, stuffing the artifact into a trouser pocket just as the beep-ing speeds up and the eerie light diffused through the flowing water shifts from yellow to red. One of the con-sole screens blinks repeatedly. *MISSILE LAUNCH, 30 SECS.*

Jae Kim almost gasps. *A launch now will surely tar-get North Korea. A counter-launch will immediately fol-low.*

Frantically, the two men begin hammering console buttons with their fists and flicking every switch in sight. There are dozens of controls to be urgently pounded and pushed. The pressure in Kim's lungs becomes a matching pounding. He is beginning to see flashes of red from the back of his eyes to match the ones pulsing from the con-trol screen.

Suddenly, the same steel table that had breached the sea wall and flooded the room shifts on its side and tilts slowly down from behind Boyd, pinning him against the top of the control panel.

Jae Kim stretches out a hand to try and pull his friend from beneath the heavy weight, but darkness starts to fill his vision. His head throbs as the countdown on the screen flicks past the designation of *:10*.

He needs air. He needs to find the kill switch. He needs to free Boyd before the man drowned.

His years of medical training and instincts for triage kick in and Kim makes the one move that he hopes will efficiently control the situation. Leaping up, his head breaks the water surface. He fills his aching chest with sweet air and dives back down to stop the missile launch.

A row of buttons hidden under a discarded clipboard has not been pressed. Kim begins pressing each one as the countdown nears *:03*. From the corner of his eye, he sees a new form lancing through the water. The readout flashes bright red, and the number on the screen reads *:01*.

Kim slams his entire right forearm against the last three buttons. The readout freezes for a second and then flashes the message, *ABORT*.

The beeping stops. Jae Kim almost exhales in excited relief. Instead, through the haze from his lack of oxygen, he barely makes out the image of his sister floating next to him and releasing Boyd's limp body from under the edge of the metal table. Darkness closes in on the scene as the controls continue to shut down.

Jae Kim's arms and legs begin to feel numb and heavy as if tied to sand bags. Gi-cho rises above him, grasping Boyd's collar and bringing him in tow toward the surface. Kim sees them fade into the darkness. The last of his air dribbles from his lips.

Abruptly, something soft yet firm presses against his

face. Air forcibly blows down his windpipe. He gasps, shocked, and opens his eyes.

His muddled awareness tells him that she is trying to give him mouth-to-mouth respiration while they were both still under water. *Impossible, child.*

She thrusts her body up and way, as Kim struggles to help her pull him above the clinging grasp of the surging sea water. Again, his head breaks the surface. Again, he sucks in the sweet air. Again, he sees Boyd's body, this time lying on the stone stairway, half way out of the rising flood.

Jae Kim's vision slowly clears. *We're not out of this yet.* He kicks off and strokes his arms in the direction of his sister and friend. The three come together for a second before stumbling up the stairs. Gi-cho helps him lift Boyd to the stone walkway that surrounded the temple grounds. Clearing the man's throat and pushing on his chest, Kim manages to get air to move in and out, but his patient remains unconscious.

There is a dark bruise on the left side of Boyd's forehead.

The rain comes again in a sudden downpour. All of the attackers are gone, but high on the hill overlooking the temple entrance, blue and red lights flash and, minutes later, police and ambulance personnel take control of the scene.

Gi-cho describes the events to a pair of officers wearing slick rain gear. A tent is thrown up over Boyd's prone form, while Kim is escorted up the hill to a waiting medical vehicle.

Someone drapes a dry blanket over his shoulders and straps to a small tank of oxygen onto his face, as his sister joins him.

A van with US Army markings pulls in next to the ambulance and several soldiers carrying firearms jump to the ground and proceed down the temple steps.

The doors of the ambulance begin to close on two patients. "Wait," Jae shouts through the breathing mask. "What about Boyd?"

The medical attendant presses him back down and tightens the safety belt on the gurney.

Almost simultaneously, Jae Kim feels overwhelmingly drained and slightly nauseous. Still, he calls out again. "What about Boyd?"

The ambulance lurches forward, wailing into the stormy night. An intense light rotates back and forth into Kim's eyes. He grasps the attendant's sleeve. "What about—"

The attendant leans back and asks Gi-cho, "Who or what is this Boyd?"

CHAPTER 16

Paris, France:

The on-off, on-off wail of police sirens echoes up through the six-story canyon streets of Paris. Miko's mind locks onto the familiar sound from years earlier.

It had been during the auto accident in Istanbul. Her car had been t-boned at an intersection, and the shock of the impact had knocked her senseless for a moment. When she'd come back to awareness, the wailing sound of the ambulance taking her to the hospital had driven itself deep into her consciousness.

There had been a brief time when she couldn't think clearly. She had lost her identity for several days and had to be institutionalized. It was a life-changing experience. She'd carefully started over, re-inventing herself, based on a few scraps of memory from her past. Birol had somehow sought her out and arranged help. She had accepted the billionaire's offer of employment, but after a time she still had occasional nightmares and sharp, sudden headaches.

The doctors had attributed her pain to a pinched disc in her upper spine. Nonetheless, Birol's trust and attraction for her had grown over the following months. And strangely so had her feelings for him.

It'd been mildly troubling, but her new life with him became an awesome success, almost a dream come true. He had given her access to personnel and security services with his growing corporations and a priceless apartment here in Paris.

Now, the siren wails fade, as Sandrine Lecombe steers the little car down the Quai Henri IV and crosses the Pont D'Austerlitz. The smell of gunpowder from the firework celebrations still hangs heavy in the night air. It drifts above the Seine, like a second ghostly river.

Something's not right. Miko questions her driver. "I thought you said we were going to your apartment on the Champs."

"Change of plans."

That's never good.

Sandrine reaches the Rue Geoffroy near the entrance to the dark and leafy Jardin des Plantes and navigates into a tiny parking space on the north side of the street. She gets out and comes around the front of the ancient Citron to open the passenger-side door. *"Allons-y, mon petit."*

The gated entrance to the jardin is closed but unlocked. As a precaution, Miko thumbs on the GPS locator hidden in the cream cameo necklace hanging under her chin. She gathers up the umbrella and follows Sandrine's clacking heels over the cobblestones, past a sleeping mongrel dog, and into the shadowy park.

At this hour, they have the place to themselves. The park, menagerie, and greenhouses had closed to the public earlier in the evening as usual, but now all the plants, shrubs and trees seem unusually quiet and even sinister.

Miko realizes she has had enough. "Stop," she called in her most commanding voice. "Where are you taking us? I've played your silly game, and now a man is dead. Where's your section of the Pandora Block?"

Sandrine continues walking as if she hasn't heard. She moves determinedly past an ancient cedar tree and up a path that leads to a yew hedge maze. In the night sky, Miko can see the skeletal structure of the iron gazebo standing at the top of the hill. She hurries ahead to block Sandrine's path. "I. Said. Stop."

They have arrived at a thatch-roofed pavilion housing a row of picnic tables and benches in the pale moonlight. Sandrine glares at her but then appears to relax, hand on hip, almost posing like a fashion model next to the door of a transgender bathroom. "I had this secreted here earlier," she smiles, reaching behind a trash bin and retrieving a soft leather pouch. The redhead dangles it from her fingertips by a pull-string strap.

Miko swallows and casts a glance around, but sees they are apparently alone. *This would be an excellent spot for an ambush.* Pausing for a moment, listening, she catches the sound of some animal housed in the nearby zoo, growling to itself. Even in the middle of her favorite city, one can find wild danger only a few feet away.

"I'm waiting," Sandrine calls, almost too confidently.

Miko takes a deep breath and with great care reaches down into the folds of the coal-black umbrella. Her fingers momentarily fumble the edge of the rolled packet placed there earlier by Gerard. Then, without a word, she hands it over. Sandrine accepts the roll of cloth in one hand and releases the leather pouch with the other. Both women open their respective packages and quickly inspect the contents.

Miko studies the L-shaped bronze piece of metal and its exotic inscription.

Sandrine unrolls the cloth sketch. A cool breeze brushes the hair on her forehead. Her smile widens as she almost whispers, "*Les juex sont faits.*"

Too late, Miko hears footsteps behind her.

Two burly men carrying truncheons and wearing badges that identified them as Europol agents advance quickly to either side of Miko.

She doesn't resist, having expected something like this from Sandrine all along. Sarcastically, she asks the clothes horse, "Where's the honor?"

Sandrine almost cackles, "Among thieves?"

It is Miko's turn to smile. "As in 'honoring a debt.' You hold my IOU and have what you asked for. Now, you have to pay what you owe me."

"I owe you nothing, bitch. And my friendly employees will help you off to prison."

One of the Europol agents turns to the other and asks in a heavy accent, "What's our play here, Vlad?"

The other agent growls, "Silence."

But Miko still doesn't let the situation intimidate her. She tells the man, "I have photographic film of that woman stealing the sketch from the Louvre." Grasping the camera strapped around her neck and unconsciously running her tongue around her teeth, she explains calmly, "This Hasselblad shoots infra-red pictures."

"But I anticipated that, *mon petit*," Sandrine snaps. "It won't do you a bit of good, because these men are in my employ."

A moment passes. Then the previously questioning agent seems confused. "I know nothing of this," he says. "Vlad told me that we were merely—"

"Sorry, madame," a new voice breaks in from behind the pavilion wall. "But *we* are in the employ of our fellow business manager, Ms. Wade."

Miko watches with satisfaction as the three security guards, she'd alerted with her cameo, take control with their raised firearms.

The Europol agents slowly lift their hands and let their truncheons clatter to the pavement.

One of Birol's guards gives Miko a two-finger salute. "We entered the grounds from the entrance beside the river and almost got turned around at the lion den."

Miko nods, snapping off another photo—this time of Sandrine fuming and holding the unrolled, stolen sketch. "And now all you need do is arrest her, gentlemen. And her friendly employees."

The three security guards take control of Sandrine's men while the irritated woman curses like a *mouille chat.*

Miko smiles. *"D'accord."* She sets the camera and umbrella on the top of the park bench and strolls casually away down the garden path. *"Touché, mon petit."*

Minutes later, exiting the park, Miko tucks the section of the Block into a pocket next to her phone and, as a final precaution, attaches the pouch to the collar of the slumbering dog. All sorts of aphorisms ramble through her mind. *Let sleeping dogs lie. You get what you pay for. Kiss my ass, sister.*

Hotwiring a Citron isn't especially hard for someone experienced in thievery. Thus, Miko drives to the Gare de Lyon and is soon onboard a TGV speeding along the tracks toward Marseilles. Still, the events of the day were unsettling. Sandrine had once been a member of Boyd's team, but from this point on, she is someone who can never be trusted again.

Even more unsettling is the new awareness Miko now has of what must have occurred during that time two years ago when she'd experienced temporary amnesia. Faint recollections now float in her mind, brought on by the blow she'd received from the heavy camera back at the Louvre. Birol had used her, unquestionably. He had even manipulated her. Why? Had he also been the cause of her auto accident years ago? Was he the root cause of the nightmares? No wonder she had felt an unsettling, unreasonable hatred for him.

But now, with her memories swirling back, she can finally explain it all. In fact, many things in her recent life which hadn't made full sense now are becoming clearer. Especially about Tim. *I've been wrong about so many things. My God, I need time to think this through.*

Hours later, seated at a sidewalk café in Marseilles, drinking a *pastise*, Miko lets the anise-flavored apéritif flow gently down her throat as she tries to relax and let the feelings ease back. She clutches the strange section of the ancient artifact and thinks of Jonathan Boyd. Taking out her phone, she presses the link to his number. Somewhere in Busan, Boyd's phone responds, but he doesn't answer.

Miko tries to concentrate, staring out at the oscillating masts of the fishing boats docked across the quai and listened to the squawking of the sea gulls. *If I wanted to, I could quit and walk away right now.*

Again she tries to reach the team's leader with her phone. No result. Uncertainty overwhelms her for a second. Should she go to Korea and try to find Boyd, or proceed to Cape Town as planned and locate Hank and his section of the Pandora Block?

She pays her bar bill and hails a cab. On the way to the Marseille Provence airport, she finally makes up her mind.

CHAPTER 17

Bogota, Columbia:

Seated in the relative comfort and safety of a se-cluded café, Louis and Tim order a second round of rye whiskey with ice. The barkeep brings the already-sweating glasses to their table where a green-and-yellow parrot ruffles its feathered wings and squawks when the man with the empty tray limps back to the bar.

The drinks are more ice than alcohol, but Tim doesn't mind at all. It helps beat the heat and quench his thirst. They've also ordered lunch, and soon are chewing soft tamales, called empanadas, filled with beef, chicken, and unidentifiable veggies wrapped up in a cornmeal sleeve.

Louis deems them "quite good, actually," but Tim thinks he detects the faint odor of armpit. *Maybe it's the parrot or the effects of the heat on my companion.*

Tim tries to use his phone to contact Miko, but the reception is intermittent at best and non-existent between times. He also tries to call Boyd's number, finally giving up in disgust. At *least, I can communicate with the barman.* He employs hand gestures to order another round.

As the meal ends, Louis pushes back his chair and stands, signaling a man just entering the café from the street. The man, suspiciously introduced by Louis as "Juan Valdez," wears a rumpled suit coat, grimy shirt open at the neck and a panama hat. A thin scar creases his left cheek from under the eye to the end of his chin, and a spider-web tattoo darkly colors the upper portion of his chest, half-hidden under a rolled scarlet bandanna. A wet cigar smolders in one side of a wide mouth. In Tim's mind, the man is something akin to a large, upright bull-frog.

"I have the transportation and special equipment you ordered ready for delivery tomorrow morning," Valdez croaks. The bulky man flashes a gold-toothed smile and exhales smoke across the table. The dank odor actually makes Tim's meal slightly tastier.

Valdez quickly advises that he cannot come along on their "expedition," but that he can direct them past the coffee plantations south of town. "No farther, you understand?"

Louis seems peeved, as only Louis can, and asks in a hushed tone about the weapons. Tim listens and learns that they will be supplied with .38 Colt revolvers for protection against "wildlife" when they begin their jungle journey.

"I'm not sure I like the sound of this entire conversation," says Tim.

"Not to worry," Louis assures him. "My old military contacts can be trusted, and we'll only need a day or two to reach our destination."

Hmmm...

The man called Valdez accepts payment for his services in the form of a roll of bills handed under the table by the Navajo warrior. Then, all three toast success to the future. The rugged Colombian flicks some ashes to the floor before standing, stretching and leaving.

Their business and drinks completed, the two North Americans wait another ten minutes and then proceed to book lodgings at a hotel across the street. Tim finds that he could relax for the first time that day, lying in their shabby room on a sagging bed under a rotating ceiling fan.

He is more tired than he realized. With the help of the cooling, hypnotic fan and a couple of bottles of warm beer, he drifts off to sleep as the sun slowly sets and an evening breeze eases the temperature down below ninety.

A distant rooster crows and Tim gropes up from a troubled slumber. He is hung over, tangled in the sheets. His mouth tastes like a sock soaked in tequila and cigar ashes. His back aches from an insistent and persistent bed spring. But he is alert after splashing water on his face and refreshed completely from a dribbling shower down the hall.

"Time to go," Louis says.

Tim follows his friend out the rear of the hotel to

where their jeep and its tarp-covered contents sit parked behind the two-story brick building. "Do we have a map, or what?"

Louis taps the side of his forehead before starting the army-surplus vehicle and putting it into gear. "Trust me," the Indian answers mysteriously. "I have a great sense of direction."

Tim moans deep in his throat, remembering a night, years ago, when they had gotten lost north of Chicago, trying to find Waukegan. He reaches down and finds the .38 Colt under his seat. Pocketing it, he replies laconically, "Indian instincts again, eh, Featherstone?"

The jeep bounds forward down an alley crowded with trash and decaying packing cases. "No," Louis laughs. "Just part of my internal radar. I find it infallible."

Now is the time for Tim to challenge his friend's confidence, but before he can, Louis adds, "And, remember, I've been here before."

Despite the uncertain circumstances, Tim feels a surge of excitement and can't help energetically calling, "Hi-oh, Silver. Away!"

Louis grimaces. "Ugh!"

For the next three and a half hours and on past noon, the two intrepid explorers travel mostly south over twisting, bumpy roads. Howler monkeys and thick, green snakes move above them in the dense foliage. Tim's stomach has just started to growl for food—or worse—when from out of the jungle, a man steps around a hillock and blocks their path.

Louis brings the jeep to a lurching halt only a couple

of feet from the man. The Navajo's hand flies to the back of the vehicle, whipping out a machete in a blur of metal. He leaps from the driver's seat and holds the long sharp-edged blade cocked menacingly above his head like a Samurai.

Tim is impressed, but the stranger isn't. In contrast to the immaculate appearance of the country's even poorest natives, this man is dirty and unwashed. His long greasy black hair and the stubble on his face fail to hide the syphilitic scars of his jaundiced complexion. Wearing baggy pants, cotton shirt and sandals, the stranger grins, showing bleeding gums and great gaps in his yellow teeth.

To Tim, the man with the red gum line looks to be a *mestizo*, a cross between Spanish and Indian, and flattering to neither group. Bleeding Gums is unarmed but doesn't seem worried about the upraised machete. A second later, Tim learns the reason for his equanimity.

"*Buenos Dias, senores,*" calls a new voice from the dense foliage.

Two more men come around the other side of the mound. The closer one has a barrel-shaped body and short arms and legs. A high Elvis-style black pompadour of thick hair surmounts a face that looks as if it could have come off a Mayan carving. He has slanted eyes, a wide blunt nose, and cruel lips like two pieces of liver. The muzzle of his semi-automatic hunting rifle is pointed in their direction. Tim wishes he were somewhere, anywhere, else.

სის

Paris, France:

Birol Kalic sits at a crystal-topped table on the balcony over-looking the Champs Elysees. The morning air is crisp, but he doesn't mind, since he wore his broad-shouldered blue suit and wide yellow tie. Later in the week, he knows his clandestine bid to purchase the old but still-reputable Cable News Network will be accepted, and half of his publicity problems will be solved.

While some consider him a corporate vampire, he felt comfortable in the position he had created as head of the Global Financial Council. He had wisely avoided employing Blacks in his many business concerns, so the Black Sea Virus had not ravaged his operations as it had other multi-national entities.

The multi-billionaire sips strong Turkish coffee and scans a report on his tablet. Three guards had been called away last night to meet with Miko Wade at the Jardin des Plantes. *What the holy hell is that about? She's supposed to be vacationing somewhere in the Caribbean. Does this relate or connect to the earlier reports of Jonathan Boyd's prison being destroyed by the invading Russians?*

Warm sunlight pours down on the front of Arc de Triomphe only two blocks away. But in Birol's mind, something is beginning to spin out of control.

He shakes his round head. Picking up one of his mobile phones, he dictates a command to his sub-chief of security. "Interrogate the three guards mentioned in report eleven-A and get back to me before the end of the day with the details of their activities. I want to know every detail of what they were doing at the park so late last night."

CHAPTER 18

Columbia:

Tim Cross occasionally has nightmares about situations like this. Well, not true nightmares. More like those rambling imaginings when you first awaken, and reality slowly pushes away at delicious fantasy, until your eyes ease open and you know you've been making stuff up in your head.

Tim often made stuff up, inner narratives where he was the heroic adventurer. Now here in the jungle of southern Colombia, he experiences the tingling thrill of being in oh-my-god, actual danger.

He holds to the idea that "a spring has no power until it's compressed." He holds to a lot of White man wet dreams like that. It is probably the results of a youth filled with comic book action, adventure, and detective stories—fun fiction that has inspired him and led him into a life-long search for the truth. Today, however, it has led him into a life-threatening standoff, and his initial reaction to the certain prospect of danger is a powerful jolt making him feel completely alive. *Hot damn!*

The third stranger moves cautiously to stand behind Elvis. He is bigger than the other two men put together. His long dark sideburns are as neatly trimmed as is his thick mustache. He is clean, and his white pants and shirt looked freshly laundered. His belly is round, but his arms and legs are muscular. He loosely holds an M-16 and wears a holstered pistol on the wide belt that supports his large gut.

Smiling pleasantly, he speaks to Louis in Spanish. The Navajo's eyes go to the M-16, and then he slowly lowers the machete and lets it fall to the ground. Without warning, Bleeding Gums steps forward and strikes Tim's friend across the face.

Louis weighs about a hundred and fifty pounds, and the blow practically lifts him off the ground and sends him sprawling into the thick grass and undergrowth. Instinctively, Tim drops his Colt but steps in between the stricken man and his assailant to ward off the kick he expects will follow. Bleeding Gums stiffens, staring at him with surprise.

Instead of cowering, Tim skewers the man with a warning glance then bends to help Louis to his feet. He is reaching for his friend's arm when his head is jerked backward as if his hair became caught in a wringer, and, for a second, he's certain his scalp will be ripped off.

Tim twists and fights for balance only to be jerked

back again. Bleeding Gums has his fingers wrapped in Tim's ginger hair. He pulls him so close that Tim practically gags on the man's fetid, oniony breath. But white-hot anger drowns out the pain. Tim relaxes slightly to gain slack and make his attacker think he is no longer resisting. His head is at an angle, and he can glimpse the man's left sandal.

Without warning, his foot comes down hard on Bleeding Gums's instep. Tim puts his whole weight into his heel, which he gyrates as if he grinding out a cigarette butt.

The man lets out a hoggish grunt and loosens his grip. Tim can see the blur of the *mestizo's* face. His elbow swings back in a short hard arc and catches the ugly man's nose and cheekbone with a satisfying crunch of cartilage. *Hot, hot, hot damn!*

Bleeding Gums yells shrilly, and Tim is at last free of the painful grip. He whirls around, as dirty fingers aim for his throat. Tim is just about to send a knee to the man's groin when—

"*Basta!*"

The big man who looks like Pancho Villa has yelled. His mouth is still smiling, but his eyes glitter with anger.

Bleeding Gums steps back, mouth still open with rage. He rubs his face, where a bruise is forming beneath the unhealthy skin. Tim takes a quick step forward, and the other man backs off. His companions howl with gales of dirty laughter.

However, Pancho Villa now seems intrigued. His eyes bore into Tim's. "Who are you?"

"Timothy Cross, American news investigator. This is my…guide." He helps Nakai off the ground. The knowing expression on Tim's face tells his friend that they might face a bleak future if these men were to know Louis's true identity. Shrugging, the Navajo adopts a groveling servile attitude.

"What are you doin' *here*?" the head man demands.

"I was informed there was a rebel base nearby. I want to conduct a few interviews. Get the truth out, you understand?"

Pancho Villa laughs. "You don't know where to go? We show you."

After a short and vocal conference, the Colombians march their captives for a few more minutes, leaving the jeep to sit in the hot jungle. Pancho leads the way. Elvis and Bleeding Gums ride shotgun behind them. They head toward a taller grassy mound where large stones are partially exposed beneath the vegetation.

Pancho walks through a corbelled arch tangled in vines and seems to disappear. Tim sees that the building houses a large orifice in the ground. They descend a flight of irregular rough-cut steps into the semi-darkness to enter a dank underground chamber with a lofty, dripping roof.

The big man speaks a few words to Louis. Then they are left alone.

"Are you all right?" Tim's voice echoes slightly.

Louis rubs the side of his face where he'd been hit. "I'll live, Timmy, but I can't say the same for the animal who struck me. And you?"

Massaging his scalp which had almost been lifted, Tim grumbles, "I think I need a haircut."

For the first time, a wide grin breaks the Indian's stony expression. "Thank you. I might have been dead if it weren't for your intervention."

"I sincerely doubt that," Tim answers without hesitation. Remembering the upraised machete, he's pretty certain that Louis would have cut Bleeding Gums down to size. "What did the big guy say?" he asked, looking back up the stairs they had come down.

"He said he wouldn't bother tying us up, since there's only one way out."

Tim looks back up the stairs they just came down. "Oh, is that all?"

"He also said they'd have someone at the entrance and, if we try to get away, they'll kill us on the spot."

Swell. Tim shrugs. "He couldn't have been any more direct than that, I guess."

"It's my fault." Louis acts glum. "I should not have brought you here along with me. The big man is the boss. The other two are just hired help, the pigs!" He pauses. "It was well that you did not say who I am."

"I didn't know how far your fame had spread. Didn't want to take a chance they knew who you are." Tim stares up at the high, dark roof, which is barely visible in the faint light coming from the entrance. "Where the hell are we?"

"It is a *cenote*, I think."

"A what now?"

"A well where the people who lived here came for

their water. Come, I'll see if I can show you what I mean."

They wander farther in for about a hundred feet. The darkness deepens and then begins to lighten again as they approach a large pool of water. Pale light streams from an opening in the rocky roof that Tim estimates must be about sixty feet above. On the far side of the wet basin, a steep wall rises to the ghostly glow of the ceiling.

The little voice in the back of Tim's mind mutters, "Things aren't going as well as planned." *We're in deep shit here. We could both die here in this darkness.*

"We have some time," Louis breaths.

Tim stares at him. "You think?"

"They will not do anything to Americans until they confer with the rest of the rebel band who hired them."

"Is that want he said? Jeez, Featherstone, nobody back in the city knows where we are."

Louis kicks a pebble into the water and watches the ripples spread away from them. "I don't think our captors know that. Still, people back in Bogota might think we've been eaten by a jaguar."

"Very funny."

"If we are lucky, we will get to meet up with some-one who remembers me here," Louis muses. "As an Indi-an, I sympathized with the basic cause of resisting an op-pressive government. Hopefully, the leader has not evolved into something less principled, like…"

"Like maybe the head of a drug cartel?" Tim rubs the back of his neck. "I can't believe that I'm doing this. I must be truly nuts. I don't know the language. I've never been here before. I'm dealing with potential killers, and I have limited combat or firearm skills."

"I would like to succeed like my brother has," Louis agrees, "but I know that my military training and track record might not be enough. We'll just have to wait and see and do our best."

"I'm chasing after a small piece of a possible cure for a terrible disease." Tim shifts his weight from one foot to the other. "I'm about as far out on a limb, as possible. Maybe, I have a death wish. Maybe I just don't care what happens any more. I drink and do dumb things, all for practically no good reason."

"Now, wait, Timmy—"

"I ought to have my head examined. Most of my old friends hate me. My old love despises me. My ex-employers won't trust or believe in my ideas. I'm a man without a job, lover, career, or any sort of good sense."

Louis comes up and shakes him by the shoulder. "Are you done?"

"I'm putting myself through all this hell for what feels like little or no reward. Why?"

"Why?"

"Because I'm stupid!"

Louis slaps him hard across both sides of the face, stunning Tim into silence. "Listen to me," the Navajo commands. "You are too easy of a mark. You fall for everything. Get control of yourself. Take charge of your future. Stand up for yourself and what you believe in."

"But, what exactly *do* I believe in?"

Louis gathers up his friend into a warm bear hug. "I

am here, Timmy, because I believe in you. Figure out what you want to get out of life—before it is too late."

From behind them, back at the entrance of the cavern, a gruff voice calls, "That is so cuddly. And disgusting."

Tim pulls away from Louis.

Pancho Villa gestures with his rifle. "Come on. Morales wants to see you."

☙❧

Minutes later, under armed guard, they are taken through a compound equipped with a target practice range, obstacle course and helicopter landing field to be presented to the well-dressed leader of the rebel forces. Bleeding Gums is there and begins to shove Tim and Louis down into a bowing posture before the leader abruptly stops him with a stern glance and swift gesture which almost spills the red wine from the glass he holds.

"Allow me," the man in charge smiles, stroking his mustache with the back of one hand. "I am Diego Morales." He wages a forefinger at them. "And I think I know one of you."

"Hola, Digger," Louis sighs. "Looks like you've finally taken over here. Where is Escobar these days?"

Morales pauses to take a sip of his wine, and Tim notices that he offered none to them. "You're old friend, Escobar, is gone. His guts carried off by the condors." He waves a casual hand up at the broad-winged birds soaring high above. "But I have missed you, *poco amigo*."

Louis seems to blush.

"Ask him about the Pandora section," Tim quietly urges his friend.

Louis nods. "I was wondering, Diego, if you still had that square piece of bronze I left behind. The one I gave to you in exchange for your silence about—"

"*Si*, I still have it. But I was planning on throwing it into the Pacific when our cartel expands again in that direction. Or maybe the Caribbean."

"Can you give it to us?" Tim finds himself grinning cheerfully, almost like a fool.

The rebel leader inspects him and purses his lips. "Is valuable to you, American, *si*? I tell you. I give it to my woman, Conchita." He shot a glance at Louis. "You remember, Conchita, eh?"

"I remember that she was Pablo Escobar's woman, before she was yours," Louis comments.

Morales tilts his head to one side like a dog in doubt. "Indeed." He directs his next words at Bleeding Gums. "Carlos, *mi confianza*, bring her here. *Rapido.*"

As the guard laughs and leaves, Morales lowers himself into a camp chair. "Sit. Sit."

Tim accepts a place on a rough-carved bench, but Louis continues to stand. "Things have changed here, Diego. The operations seem a lot more military than when I left months ago."

"Ah," Morales responds, again waging his finger. "It has been more than a year, *poco*. You left here in 2018 before we took on the Syrian contract. Escobar had us sinking in the *arenas movedizes* of drug trafficking back then."

"Movie days?" Tim asks.

"Quicksand," Louis defines.

Morales sets his wine glass on a table half covered with map rolls. *There's that smile again, like looking down the barrel of a gun.*

The leader stands, facing the Navajo. "Now, we make *mucho dinero* teaching others how to fight against oppression."

CHAPTER 19

Syrians? Here in south America?" Tim comes to his feet. It seems the popular thing to do. "This is a training camp? For which side?"

"The paying side," Morales leers, touching his mustache again. "We're growing up and prosperous, eh?"

Or down. There is a story here, and Tim's investigative instincts kick in. Someone had once told him that many of the Spanish who populated the New World where of Muslim-decent from Iberia. As recently as a hundred years ago, Syrian-Lebanese immigrants established large Arabic-speaking populations in cities like Bogota. Now, it appears that Middle East terrorist groups might be coming here to hone their military skills where the world would never think to look for them. Tim wonders how and if he'll ever be allowed to file this exclusive.

Bleeding Gums returns with a grunt, walking behind

the woman he's been sent to retrieve. She is younger than Tim expected and wears some sort of leather sleeve on her right forearm. If she had been with the rebels years earlier, as Louis mentioned, then she must have been in her teens at the start. Now, with wide hips and full breasts captured in men's work clothes, she gives the impression of someone who could lead this motley band, given half a chance.

She approaches Morales, head held high.

"Conchita." He reaches back and slaps her across the face with a crack that makes Tim wince. The impact brings blood to the side of her mouth.

Then again, she'll never lead anyone if she puts up with crap like that. Tim takes a step forward, ready to confront the situation.

Louis clutches his shirt sleeve. "Hey, be careful, buddy. Do not go all Chris Pine on me."

"Who?"

"You know. Chris Pine. He plays the hot and heroic Captain Kirk in the movies."

Tim scowls. *That didn't sound right.* He shrugged, demanding, "Can you give us the bronze artifact, or not?"

The woman reaches down into the front left pocket of her jeans and tosses Tim a wad of newspaper. It is a page torn from his own paper, *The Gazette,* and it contains a ten-millimeter square bit of dull gold metal with inscribed scratches on two sides.

Louis leans over to catch a glance. "Yep, that is the true item."

Tim palms it, looking up. "What'll it cost us?"

"You can keep it," Morales smiles, bowing from the hips. "It is my gift—because you are not ever going to leave here, *mi amigos*."

Now Louis steps forward. "Look, Digger. If you think you can—"

The rebel leader cuts him off with a swiping gesture that automatically brings semi-automatic weapons up and at the ready from two guards.

The high altitude makes breathing hard enough for Tim, without this new threat of gunfire.

Morales continues to taunt them. "I don't go by that name any longer. Would you like the grand tour of the compound?"

Tim eyes the business ends of the rifles. *Stay calm.* "Do we have a choice?"

"I will take them," the woman says, shoving past Bleeding Gums. "Come."

Louis and Tim exchange looks and then follow the female in jeans.

Outside, beyond the crackling firing range where dozens of rag-tag troops sharpen their skills with automatic weapons, Conchita marches along a barbed-wire fence and tosses words over her shoulder. "You are dead men, you know."

This time, Louis's expression is unreadable. *If he's not going to panic, I'm not either.*

They continue to follow the woman as she adds, "And so am I. These are not my people."

Tim begins to understand. "I think it's time to play 'Let's Make a Deal.'"

Louis shoots him an insane expression.

Tim picks up the pace, coming around the woman to speak directly to her in a low voice. "Is there someplace we can talk? And maybe get a drink?"

She nods slightly. "We can talk while we walk, but keep it quiet."

"Roger."

"I was sympathetic to anti-government rebels fighting against oppression," Conchita murmurs, "but this site has turned into a mercenary camp based only on pure greed."

"I can see that," Tim agrees.

"Ex-drug loads training terrorists," Louis muses. He nudges his companion. "Hell of a story, eh, Timmy?"

"We have what we came for," Tim answers, turning his head to see if they were being followed. "I say that we all get out while we can."

A shadow crosses their path from one of the large birds soaring on high.

The woman waves her leather-strapped arm at the creature. The enormous bird eases lower in their direction but sails off, as if offended by the presence of the two strange men.

"I have to get away," she says in a confidential tone. "I've learned that my sister may be infected by the virus."

Louis clears his throat. "You know," he comments while casually strolling around the front end of a mud-splattered Humvee, "the condor appears on the official state seal of seven different countries down here." The Navajo pops the squat vehicle's hood.

"The people of Latin America all think alike," Conchita replies, watching Louis fiddle with starter controls. "Especially when it comes to basic symbols."

Tim goes along with the nonchalant performance. "Looks like a big vulture to me." A trickle of sweat rolls down his spine.

Conchita wets her lips nervously, as Louis gets the engine started. Within seconds, she and Tim pile in to sit beside the Navajo, who grounds a gear and gooses the hulking, open-topped vehicle forward.

Louis steers off the dirt road and aims the Humvee directly down a sloop. "Get down, or you'll be sliced to pieces!" They plow through the multi-strand barbed-wire fence.

Tim ducks beneath the low dash. *Jeez, that was close!* He catches sight of the woman huddled low in the back seat as the car bounces over a rut and swerves around a tangled clump of jungle growth. It is a good thing that they were hunkered down, because a series of high-powered shells whiz over their heads and fracture the windshield, from behind.

A familiar exhilaration runs through Tim as he realizes his life is once again in danger. An urge to grab the wheel away from Louis is almost overpowering.

Within seemingly seconds of their barrowing through the compound's perimeter, twin helicopter gunships rise above their heads carrying what appears to be a crew of three and a ventral-mounted, swiveling twenty-millimeter cannon.

"Find some cover! Now!"

There is little Louis can do to evade the chopper, except try to take the Humvee off the road into the densest part of the jungle.

The pilots of the assault helicopters play a smart game. Their twenty-millimeter shells rip through the upper levels of the tree tops and pepper the earth all around the fleeing vehicle. Both the left fender and passenger-side door of the Humvee suddenly shatter and fly off into the dark, thick tangle of emerald vines. The murderous but inaccurate fire sprays all around, piercing thick branches and leaves, slicing brilliant orchids to confetti-like shreds.

Louis throws the four-wheel-drive into a sharp ninety-degree turn, skirting around a protruding rocky slope that successfully blocks off the storm of shell fire.

Almost simultaneously, the humid jungle air becomes quiet. The choppers have pulled away.

That is when Tim sees the bleeding wound on the side of Louis's head. *Crap! Crap!*

His friend's sad eyes don't seem to focus. His mouth trembles as he speaks. "Timmy…"

Tim desperately searches for something to wrap around his friend's head to stench the flow of blood. He tears his own shirt open, pulling it from his shoulders and catching a sleeve beneath his shoe. He yanks upward until the seam rips, giving him a couple of feet of cloth to wind around Louis's wound.

As the woman helps him manipulate the wounded Navajo into the back seat, a new sound filters through the overhanging vegetation.

An angry buzzing sound.

"Shit!" Tim bounces into place behind the wheel. "They've got drones!"

Once again, he feels the childish thrill of danger course through his veins. *Hot damn, this is insane!* From the seat behind him, he hears Louis call out something about "Mrs. Cross's little boy."

Tim stomps the accelerator pedal, ramming the vehicle through a wall of lush foliage. His intent is to mask their location among the thicker mass of jungle growth, but he only succeeded in capturing the damaged front end in a snarl of thick vines. An equally thick snake tumbles down from a branch and flops into Conchita's lap. She shrieks, heaving it away, unfortunately onto Tim's right thigh. *Cri—ist!*

The buzzing grows louder, accompanied by the sound of rapid fire. Tim shrugs the snake away. "The drones have teeth," he yelps.

The Humvee jolts up and over a rotting tree trunk, kicking Louis's body almost out of the back, if they hadn't strapped him in with the seat belts.

"Go that way," Conchita shouts, straight-arming the dashboard and pointing past Tim's face to a bright area off to their left.

"Are you nuts? That's open country. They'll find us for sure out there."

"Do it!" the woman howls. "Once we're in the open, I can get us help."

Shaking a shower of sweat from his head, Tim angles the low car out into a field of shoulder-high grass.

Do it. Do it. Yeah, I can do it. The baking sun burns down as the growing specks in the sky began to zero in on them. Small-caliber bullets zip past from on high. One, two, three clang into the rear of the Humvee to no effect. *The drones will have the range in seconds.*

One of the flying weapons zooms in from the left and levels off in front of the moving car. Tim wrenches the wheel over, swerving away and almost striking a van-sized rock hidden in the tall grass.

The first drone tilts and swoops after them, lining up its sights again on the front of the Humvee. Tim jerks the steering wheel in the other direction, thinking that he should never have driven out in the open. "We're going back into the jungle before we get shot to shit!"

In response, Conchita, at last, kicks the snake out through the gaping passenger-side opening, puts her fingers into her mouth, and lets out a high-pitched whistle. Within seconds, the ten-foot span of a condor swishes past. The bird's lowered claws grasp the drone like helpless prey, carrying it up and away, before flinging the damaged device into the side of another massive stone.

Tim glances sharply at Conchita whose face is stern and eyes searching. "Hell of a trick, lady."

She lets loose with another whistle, just as the second drone buzzes in like a jet fighter from their right side. A round from the thing's firearm tears past Tim's shoulder and impacts into the odometer. Then the giant bird's dark shadow flickers over them again. The drone is shattered, spinning into the branches of a distant tree, sending screeching monkeys scattering in a panic.

Conchita watches and then smiles. "I told Diego that those things were no match for my birds."

"I take it all back," Tim exhales, shaking the strain and adrenaline rush from his shoulders. "I *love* those beautiful birds. What a great symbol of strength and power!"

Three minutes later, they are back on the dirt road. The sun is lowering as they reach an intersection of crumbling paved highway. Conchita instructs him to hide the Humvee in a vine-filled gully.

"Louis needs medical help," Tim argues.

Without another word, the woman yanks the wheel over, sending the vehicle into the thick foliage.

"Dammit," Tim shouts, almost falling out of the driver seat, "On foot, they'll find us for sure."

Conchita slips out from her side of the Humvee. "There's a daily bus is due by here at any minute."

Better be right about that, lady. Stepping back toward the pavement with Louis in tow, Tim catches sight of an orange and rust-brown public conveyance churning toward them from down the road. "You okay, Featherstone?"

Louis smiles weakly. His eyes focus on the tuft of ginger hair on Tim's naked chest. "Looking very buff, Timmy. Like you always say, 'Fine as the hair on a frog.'"

Tim grunts, "Well, not exactly." He heaves his buddy forward. "Let's get you to a doctor."

Conchita waves her leather-strapped arm. The bus screeches to a halt, and they stumble aboard.

Tim eyes the driver and wordlessly forks over a wad of pesos. They fumble down the aisle and collapse into a row of seats near the back. A young boy tries to sell them meat pies and soda pop from a plastic bucket. He looks no more than ten and has a hoarse voice, bruised face and scabby legs. Again, money is exchanged, and Tim is soon wearing the boy's sweat-stained shirt and cane hat.

Most of the passengers are women, with white dresses sporting colorful embroidered patterns. Even a small girl carries a beaded purse clutched in her tiny hands.

Conchita leans in to Tim and starts to explain. "This is obviously a singing troupe from the local mission. It is good that we are not…"

Tim hears the woman speaking, but his mind is still on the chase through the Colombian jungle. He tries to remember when he'd been involved in anything so dangerous and again considers the possibility that he might have a death wish. *I could have been killed. What's wrong with me? There's too much at stake to be fooling around like that.*

"Are you listening to me?" Conchita shakes his shoulder. "This is where we get off. The hospital is over there next to the parking garage."

Tim realizes, with a touch of embarrassment, that he has been tuning her out. "Oh, okay. That's good." He gets up and helps Louis to his feet. "Come on, pal."

When he turns around, the woman kisses him on the cheek. "This is where I leave you. Good luck! I must find my sister." He blinks and watches her slip into the crowded street. He vaguely recalls Conchita saying something during the bus ride about her sister contracting the virus. He wants to help her—he owes her his life—but he knows he has to get Louis to a doctor.

Louis moans and has trouble staying on his feet. The crowd of Columbian pedestrians flows on and away.

Tim curses under his breath. At the back of his mind lurks the thought that the virus might have jumped to another race. He devoutly hopes not. *I've got to get back in contact with Boyd and Miko. ASAP.* Moving into the hospital, where English is freely spoken, he takes some comfort in thinking that their assignments surely must have been a less dangerous than his.

The small emergency room is mobbed with grumbling patients, most of who appear to fear that they are infected by the Black Sea Virus. Pregnant women sit uncomfortably in unpadded metal chairs, waiting for treatment, hoping for a cure.

After an hour that tests his patience, Tim finally gets a physician to flash a light into Louis Nakai's eyes. The doctor pronounces the Navajo healthy enough to leave the clinic after consuming a handful of pink, pain-reliever tablets. But Louis refuses to ingest the drugs, until Tim convinces him that, in this case, it would be a proper idea to "augment his awareness."

After what we've just been through, I could use an attitude adjustment, myself. Maybe two or three.

At a nearby bar that has plenty of beer and no parrots, they sit at a rickety table, and Tim tries to call Miko. No answer.

Louis taps a number into the cell phone and makes

contact with Juan Valdez. They arrange for their transportation back to the Bogota airport. Tim is still certain that something's still going to go wrong. *Wait for it. Wait for it.*

Once in the taxi, he asks to have a look at the Pandora Block section they have acquired. Rotating it in his fingertips, he inspects its shiny surface. *What a cryptic enigma!* "It's like putting Humpty Dumpty back together again."

Louis smiles from under his bandaged forehead. "Did you know that in the original poem, there is no mention of eggs?"

"Are you sure you're feeling all right?"

"I'm okay. When we get to the airport, where are we going?"

"We should meet up with the rest of the old team," Tim replies. "I tried to call Miko, but she doesn't answer."

"What about calling our old boss, Boyd. This is his show, right?"

"Tried that, too. No answer."

"Let me see your phone again."

Tim hands it over and watches the city slide past outside the taxi window. Far to the west, the setting sun paints the undersides of the clouds in hues of orange, red and purple. *It's still hotter than hell, but I'm getting used to it.*

"Here." Louis hands back the mobile device. "I have tracked her phone via its GPS. Looks like she is in Cape Town, South Africa."

Tim gazes at the screen, somewhat relieved. "Makes sense. That's where we're supposed to meet up with Hank Jones."

"Jeez. That's not good. The majority of people in Cape Town are Black. The virus must be running rampant there."

Tim takes a deep, settling breath, the first in a long time. "We'll see."

CHAPTER 20

It had been agreed that, after Boyd, Tim, and Miko completed their missions and retrieved their sections of the Block, they would all meet to collect the seventh and final piece in Cape Town.

Having charged his phone during the plane ride, Tim reads Miko's belated message. *The city is suffering through rolling blackouts. I'm on my way to Hank's jazz club near the soccer stadium.* He quickly Googles info about the city, figuring he better learn as much as possible. *The last thing Louis and I need is to get lost.*

The two travelers land at Cape Town International airport twenty minutes later, dog tired but determined to join up with the rest of the team.

The trip has taken a full twenty-four hours through Sao Paulo, Brazil, and Johannesburg, and now they find

South Africa to be in full crisis. The BSV has hit the country hard, killing thousands of pregnant women, mostly in populated areas, like Cape Town. Hospitals have been over capacity for months.

The World Health Organization has set up seven different treatment centers to handle the emergency, but they are unable to keep back the demand and panic. Two large medical ships are anchored in Table Bay, full to capacity. Riots break out daily from anger, the desperate need for food and the general fear that the black race has been cursed by God.

Tim and Louis's cab ride along Route 2 to M6 is interrupted twice by speeding ambulances and police vans. After more than thirty-five minutes, they finally arrive at their destination between the waterfront and Signal Hill, nine miles west of the airport. It is a two-story strip mall near the donut-shaped stadium located in the Green Point area off Granger Bay Boulevard. Just after eight-thirty in the evening, they enter the Blue Train jazz club and find Jae Kim and a young oriental woman listening to Hank Jones finger and cajole a cool Coltrane number from a battered saxophone.

Tim rushes to greet the Korean, whom he hasn't seen in years, and to order a double scotch. While Jae Kim and Louis pat each other on the back, the young woman waits to be introduced.

"Timmy, this is my sister, Gi-cho," the medical researcher grins. "Don't get any ideas."

Tim accepts the woman's slim hand and gives Jae a raised eyebrow. "I knew that family was important to you, but I didn't think you haul one of them around with you."

Jae Kim shakes his head. "Believe me, pal. It was not my idea." They all grab chairs and huddle around the small table as the sax number ended. "What happened to him?" Jae gestures with his chin at the Navajo's head. "Why the bandage?"

"He got winged while we chased down his piece of the puzzle in Colombia."

"Colombia? But I thought—"

"Long story. Boyd or Miko here?"

The broad-shouldered, coffee-colored man who has been playing Coltrane comes over. He looks to be in his mid-fifties, six-feet tall and running to fat. "Miko Wade? Is she coming, too?"

Louis half-rises from his seat at the table. "Hey, Hank."

"Sit down, scag." The black man with the thick and even blacker mustache almost growls. "You're lucky I let you in here."

Louis sinks back down calmly enduring the insult while lightly touching his wounded head. Hank's harsh gaze burns down at him. In Tim's mind, Boyd's caution-ary words about the two men still echo. *'Keep those two apart. They're like a match and gasoline.'*

Jae Kim accepts a glass of Gibson from their waiter and raises it in Hank's direction. "Here's to the man who owns the place."

Tim smiles. "Then the drinks are on the house, right?"

Hank doesn't flinch. "Wrong, traitor."

"Uh, let us not get into that now." Louis scratches his nose. "Where is Boyd? This is his puzzle party."

"We don't know," the Korean woman answers. "We had some difficulty getting our part of the block and haven't been able to locate him since."

"Sounds like Boyd to me," Hank tells them, still standing. He seems more comfortable on his feet than letting himself relax. "How many pieces have we got?"

The group exchanges glances. "I gave mine to Boyd," Tim said, finishing his scotch. "So, we've only got Jae's and—"

"The gay Indians," Hank grunts.

Louis purses his lips. For a second Tim thinks Louis is going to blow Hank a kiss. "Yes. And we'd have mine, Boyd's and Miko's, too, if they were here."

A firm voice behind them at the entrance to the club calls, "I'm here." Miko Wade weaves her way through the crowded tables and comes up to rest a hand on Louis's right shoulder.

"Hey, lady," the Navajo laughs.

Hank sort of bows from the waist and neck. "Miko."

Jae Kim gets up and offers a hand.

Gi-cho and Tim remain silent, watching, for different reasons.

Tim remembers when they parted at the St. Thomas airport and thinks, "She looks even better than before."

Miko releases Jae Kim's hand. "We never actually met, back in the day, but I heard a lot about your dramatic performances, on and off the stage."

The Korean blushes. "Yes, we were always on different assignments. But it's a great pleasure to finally meet you in person."

Louis sets his drink down and stares at Jae. "You had an acting career?"

The medical man's blush has faded. "It was more like stand-up. Don't forget to tip your waitress."

Another round of drinks arrives, but Tim resolves to show the group that he is all business. He leans in to capture Miko's attention. "Have you got Sandrine's section?"

She dusts away an imaginary crumb from the table top. "Of course. Although it wasn't any walk in the park."

Louis swirls his drink. "Where is she?"

"She's—been detained." Then Miko shifts shoulders to stare at Tim. "And I owe you an apology."

He drops his gaze. "What…uh…for?"

"Something I…remembered."

Tim rotates his glass on the table with his fingertips. "Go on."

"Don't play or push me, okay?" she snaps.

The rest of the group waits for a response. They all know of Miko and Tim's past relationship.

"Okay. I won't," he drawls. "But I tried to reach you. Boyd, too."

"Where is he?"

"We don't know." He looks to Jae Kim, who nods agreement. "I can't reach him either."

"Great." She takes Tim's glass from his hand and finishing off the drink. "I'm sure he'll show up, eventually."

Tim holds back a chuckle. "He always does."

Their eyes lock, as he watches her throat as she elegantly swallows. *Toying with me, like old times. I like it, but why?*

"So what do we do now?" asks Miko.

It surprises him that she trusts him enough to ask for his opinion. *Oookay. I guess I can handle this. Sure, why not?* "First, I think Jae should look after Louis's injury. Then we need to put the pieces together and see what we've got."

Miko pushes back from the table. "Oh, so you think you're in charge again now?"

Tim feels his neck stiffen. *Yep, definitely toying with me.* "Well, certainly not you, Mik. We're all a team again, and we should act like one. You've been bossing people around with Birol for far too long."

Miko's eyes and the line of her mouth tighten. "Is that a fact?"

Louis raises a palm. "Wait, guys—"

Miko ignores the Indian code-cracker. "Or is that the booze talking, Timbo?"

Gi-cho offers a cautious comment. "I am enthused to be considered part of this dynamic team."

Everyone stares at her until she again looks down, fingertips at her lips.

"Right." Hank nods, moving away. "We can continue this discussion somewhere less public. Y'all come with me, now. Da Black Fox and I live in the back behind the bar."

"The Black Fox?" Miko asks. They pass behind the curtains of the foot-high performance stage and enter a doorway concealed there.

"My woman. She's pregnant," he says solemnly. "We need to work fast."

⌘

As they enter the room, the lights flicker, but they can all see the woman lying on the couch, wearing earphones and watching a video on an iPad. Her belly is swollen, and perspiration dots her forehead and broad upper lip.

The video appears to be the latest news about the virus outbreak and instructions for pregnant women to check themselves into a clinic for government treatment.

"The blackout will hit here in a couple of minutes," Hank says, going around the room, lighting candles. "Honey, this is my old crew from when we were exposing injustice."

The woman's eyes scan the group. "I don't need justice. I need pain killers."

Jae Kim immediately approaches her, searching through the pockets of his coat. "I'm a medical researcher and have oxy, if that will help." He looks around to the others, without embarrassment. "Maybe, ma'am, we could go…say…into the bedroom and I could examine your condition."

As the two walk together as one into a back room, Tim hears Miko say, "It's been half a decade since I've seen any of you devils."

Hank responds philosophically with, "Five years is a long time, these days."

"A lot has changed," she agrees.

Tim looks at Miko. *How is she taking it?*

There is an expectant silence, broken by a painful moan from the other side of what Tim figures is the bedroom door.

Louis pipes up with, "Tim's a reporter, now."

"Doesn't look mild-mannered to me," Hank grunts. His eyes are full of concern, trained on the closed door. His voice is flat. "I work as a forensic anthropologist at a local university. Or at least I did before all the deaths and riots started."

Tim picks up the conversation. "It's okay, big guy. Take it easy. Jae Kim's a full doctor, researching the cure."

Hank's face stays stony. "I see Louis has come completely out."

"Of the closet?"

"No. Out of his thick Indian skull. What did you think I meant?"

Louis lightly touches the bandage on his head. "I like this little club you're running. Seems very cozy. And gay."

Hank doesn't answer. It is clear that he is holding himself in check.

The silence becomes oppressive, until Miko comments, "I think you all know that I've been working of Birol Kalic. In security."

"I saw you on television." Tim couldn't help adding, "Although, I couldn't tell if the story was about security or securities."

Gi-cho makes a questioning face, but keeps quiet.

Miko's tone is chilling. "I run his body guards."

Hank almost smiles. "With that body, honey, I bet you give them a hell of a run."

Miko winks at him. "I can slap you to death, six different ways."

Louis laughs at that, just as Jae Kim comes back into the room.

They all look at him expectantly.

"She's resting quietly now," he tells Hank.

"Thanks, Doc," the big man answers. "I guess I'm glad you're all here."

Jae rests a hand on Hank's shoulder and then pushes gently past him. "Okay, Louis, you're next. Let's have a look that that head injury."

The Navajo again touches the patch at his temple. "It's not bad."

∽∾∽

Jae Kim inspects Louis's wound. "I'm sorry to say that this looks bad." The skin above the eyebrows has darkened to a gun-metal blue. "I'm sure you have a hematoma. We need an MRI."

"I'll be all right. Hank's the one we should be worried about, or his wife anyway."

Kim grimaces. "I just don't know any more."

Louis reaches and holds close the other man's shirt front. "Look, I can do this. And so can you. Don't go giving up on us. We all did a lot of bad things in the past, but forget all that. This is our big chance to make up for any failure."

Kim's eyes nearly brim. "You're right, of course." He clears his throat. "For my family's sake, I need to up my game."

The Navajo smiles and then winces from the resulting pain. "I trust you, Doc. So, quit feeling sorry for yourself."

Again Tim looks in Miko's direction. *What a tough little guy.* "Okay. What say we start getting that block built?"

CHAPTER 21

I've got the section," Hank had said an hour earlier, "or at least I know where it is."

The visiting members of the group have checked into a small motor lodge near the sports stadium. It is decided that Jae Kim and his sister will continue to minister to Hank's wife and keep a close eye on Louis's condition.

The Navajo's speech has started to slur occasionally. "Might be the effects of the alcohol," Kim advises, "but it's best to be cautious."

Now in the early morning just before dawn, Miko uneasily joins Tim in shadowing Hank to the location where the seventh piece of the Pandora Block can be retrieved. They sit inside an extended van outside the Green Point Stadium parking garage, watching the screen of a laptop computer Louis has linked to the few security cameras still functioning inside the unused sports arena.

Years ago, the stadium had been filled to capacity

with cheering spectators from around the world eager to see the 2010 World Cup semi-final match between Uruguay and the Netherlands. At that time, Hank had been studying archeology, assisted by his uncle who was part of a group of South Africans known then as the Black Atlantis Society. It was a harmless social group of locals, based on the view that mankind's origins stemmed from the northern regions of the continent.

Hank shifts uneasily in his seat within the van. "My uncle believed that all of the races of man came from an island in the Black Sea. He was a highly-respected archeologist at the time and got me interested in the field of ancient languages, as I was growing up. That was before his theories were considered to be without value by the academia."

Tim crosses his arms. "I remember the story now. His theories were discredited at the time."

"Yes. It hit him hard, but he never stopped believing that all mankind came originally from Atlantis. Especially, the Black race."

Tim's reporter instincts perk up. "There appears to be growing proof that he may be right about that."

"And a growing chance that my wife may be cured," Hank says with a mixture of grudge and hope.

Miko urges them on. "If we can get that last piece back from the society and translate the inscription—at least, that was Boyd's plan."

"That's still a big if." Tim sighs.

Hank thinks out loud. "We'll get it back. The society has grown reluctant to operate openly in public, but I'm certain I can negotiate the return from them. My uncle will listen to his favorite nephew—if I go alone."

Due to the devastating effects of the virus, there hasn't been a sporting event scheduled at the stadium in over a year. The parking garage is blocked off to vehicles, but an individual can easily walk through the entrance, past the abandoned cashier's booth. Hank follows the painted yellow arrows down to the lowest level. The cavernous space is empty except for a single black van parked next to a concrete pillar. "There must be a back entrance that they've discovered," Hank thought, scoping out the surroundings.

Ranks of numbered pillars support the low ceiling. A few fluorescent lights banish the shadows from the site. The air is warm and humid. The vacant lot manages to feel both spacious and claustrophobic at the same time. Noise from the city above fails to penetrate the sepulchral stillness of the underground garage. Hank's footsteps echo hollowly against the dense concrete walls.

Above, Tim and Miko have located the stadium's security office and managed to coax a few of the video cameras into operation. Everyone on the team had agreed that it would be best if Hank alone met with his uncle and the BAS. No one wanted to queer the deal or spook the society.

But after seeing the group of men gathered in the parking area next to the black van, Hank's concern begins to rise. Up top-side, where the images are transmitted to the laptop, Miko is disturbed to find that the security cameras are clouded from grime and auto exhaust accumulated on the surfaces of the lens. *One working screen is completely blurred.* "Probably a spider web," she mumbles to Tim.

The silent views create a sensation of watching a broadcast emanating from under water. The deep shadows drifting from the far recesses of the garage add to the eerie view.

Hank's back is to the camera on the lower level. He comes on mid-screen, joined by a handful of blurred figures.

"Are they wearing robes?' Tim asks, squinting. He begins to feel the old excitement building up inside him, ready to charge through his veins.

"Will you relax, already?" Miko chides.

It is irksome that she insists on mocking and even rejecting his opinions, but regardless of her sarcastic comment, Tim remains determined to do what he feels is right.

Miko doesn't care for Tim's childish recklessness, but she does have a strong desire to save lives, no matter how strange the circumstances. She has almost always gone along with Tim's nonsense, grudgingly, on principle. Essentially, they are on a stake out, just like years earlier when running their confidential investigations ops in Los Angeles. Only this time, they are older and—in her case—wiser.

Nonetheless, she senses a growing unease, watching the muddled figures on the computer screen. Yet she wants Tim to see that she appears confident. *Big girl panties.* "This should only take a minute or two."

☙☙☙

Hank shakes his head and fights the urge to put a palm to his face. It's damn-right silly to be meeting his uncle here like this. But the situation is deadly urgent, so he resigns himself to play his part. He deliberately pushes his doubt aside and again asks, "Did you bring that little bronze section of the block that I asked for?"

His uncle hesitates.

"We have a better idea," says one of the men in the huddled group.

Hank does not recognize the speaker, and he certainly doesn't like his tone.

Then, his uncle's voice holds an edge of suspicion. "Why do you want the Atlantian artifact?"

Hank automatically widens his stance, as if his body is unconsciously preparing for a confrontation—which it is. "When I gave it to you, I had no idea that it might be part of a relic containing a cure for the virus."

"A cure for the BSV?" his uncle inquires.

"Do you have the other parts that go with it?"

Again, Hank can't tell which of the half-dozen men is speaking.

At a gesture from his uncle, two of the men come closer.

Hank focuses on controlling the situation, as well as his feelings. "My friends have them," he starts to explain. "We need the remaining piece to complete the artifact and get—"

"We want the complete artifact," his uncle interrupts.

"You will remain with us until your friends deliver it."

I was afraid of this. Hank puts his hands up, as if to push back on the group's intent. "Now, wait—"

Above, watching through the muddy camera views, Tim says, "This looks bad. Wish we could hear them."

Miko reacts with growing alarm. "They're surrounding him and moving toward the van."

"I don't like this," Tim yelps. *Not good!* "We need to go get him."

"Look!" She points at the laptop image. "He's staring into the camera. They don't see his face."

Tim leans over, straining to see every detail on the screen, hoping for a clearer view. "I think he just said, 'Table Bay' and something else. What's a table bay?"

"They're shoving him toward that car. Must intend to take him with them somewhere." Miko switches to a web browser and Googles "Table Bay." It's that body of water northeast of here."

Tim chews on the edge of his lower lip. "Sounds right. I think I saw something about that when we landed." He watches Hank's form enter the back of one of the dark vehicles. "Try looking up 'Jolly Roger Pirate Boat.'"

"The what now?"

"That's the other thing I think he mouthed at the camera." Tim feels doubtful of his own words and adds, "I think."

The figures on the screen have all moved into the black SUV. A tiny image in the corner of Miko's computer screen shows the vehicle moving out of view.

"Yes. Here it is." She almost gasps. "Jolly Roger is a

tourist attraction on the waterfront about a mile from here. You can rent the boat and party there on the bay in the sunset each evening."

"Come on." Tim climbs into the driver's seat. "Let's see if we can get there in time."

"In time for what?"

"In time for what...ever." He makes a confused expression and starts the engine.

Miko's French automatically takes over. "In time for...*merde*."

∗∗∗

The virus morphs and mutates, mindlessly. Soon it will have a transference vector into a larger pool of tissue. The urge to expand pulses, growing, differentiating, morphing hungrily for new life to control.

∗∗∗

When operating under intense stress, Miko and Tim think a lot alike. They both quickly conclude that their best option for retrieving both Hank and the final section of the Pandora Block requires a direct approach. Following the directions acquire from the website, Tim steers the van into a parking place behind a combination ship's chandler and souvenir shop. Miko phones Jae Kim to let him know what has developed and that they are now located on the waterfront.

The fake pirate ship sits low in the water at the dock

between a catamaran and a small yacht. The air holds a tang of brine and fish. A morning mist still shrouds the upper reaches of Table Top Mountain which sits solemnly behind and above the city, overlooking the harbor. At this early hour, few people are near the docks, especially tourists who might have planned a lively fishing or drinking trip for later that day.

The sixty-foot, three-masted ship is painted brown to suggest a wooden hull and sports a black-and-white skull and crossbones fluttering in the mild ocean breeze. The snouts of black plastic cannons poke out from the port side of the vessel, and a figurehead of a large-breasted mermaid stares proudly into space. The ship's masts are rolled up, probably permanently, and the gangway is chained off. But that doesn't stop the group of men who crowd around Hank.

Tim immediately calculates that they are two football fields away from the group. *Maybe I can rush them and get to Hank.* Even though he can almost hear the trill of excitement charging along his spine, recent events have proven to him that he is woefully out of shape. *Or maybe not.*

It is during the act of sliding around the rear of a buttoned-up food truck for Mamma Mandela's Lemon Ice that Tim realizes they have made a critical error. The collective members of BAS have easily spotted Miko and Tim coming toward them. The group begins to hurriedly hustle along the quai to duck under the chains and up the gang plank.

Tim guesses that one of the men has control or a

vested interest in the fake three-master. He took a guess and told Miko, "They might be planning to hold Hank here," he decides out loud. "Until they can get the other sections of the block."

Easing carefully forward to avoid any impression of aggression, Miko answers from the side of her mouth, "How do you figure?"

"Hank said that his uncle and the other BAS guys were fanatics about Atlantis. I think they're going to hold him until we bring them the other pieces."

Miko shakes her head ruefully. "And I think you always see nutty conspiracies where there are none. Come on and keep your thoughts to yourself." *Where does he get this stuff?*

Before them, the gaily-painted faux pirate ship lists slightly to starboard as the cluster of men clambered aboard. Out in the bay, a distant cruise ship fires a cannon shot that sends a flock of gulls squawking across the small harbour. The puff of white smoke and accompanying *boom* takes everyone by surprise.

Hank sags in the arms of his captors, grimaces and puts his hands to his chest.

Tim and Miko edge closer and stand on the dock at the end of the gangway. The group of men around Hank becomes confused. Some back away, while others bend closer to their captive.

Miko hears a whimpering voice call out, "My heart."

With trembling hands, their friend fishes a plastic pill container from his pocket. His palsied fingers struggle with the safety cap.

One of the BAS men on the boat—probably Hank's uncle—shouts, "Call an ambulance!"

Tim pulls out his phone. *Is Nine-One-One the correct emergency number in South Africa?*

Miko tugs at his arm, interrupting. "I've seen him do this before."

Tim looks back up. "Oh?"

With a groan and convulsive motion, Hank wrenches open the pill container, only to lose his grip on the vial. Dozens of purple capsules spill out onto the wooden deck. "My medicine!"

The men kneel down and begin frantically trying to capture and scoop up the scattered pills.

Hank makes eye-contact with his two friends and nimbly breaks from the group to dash down the gang plank and jump the chain before joining them in a brief run behind the food truck.

"Pretty neat," Tim comments in genuine admiration. They dodge between a row of dumpsters and a sleeping homeless man. The BAS men are shouting and not far behind.

Hank shares a wide grin and opens his left fist to show Tim the jagged bit of metal that is his section of the block. "Picked my uncle's pocket, too. You all know I'm the best thief on the team."

Miko huffs, "Aside from Boyd." They sprint along the wharf past the Waterfront Boat Company.

Tim becomes winded again. Miko and Hank are getting ahead of him, over coiled ropes and painted pylons. He pushes himself forward with a new burst of speed and stumbles into Hank before going down and skinning his left knee on the dock.

The small piece of bronze-colored metal flies from Hank's hand and plops into the dark, oily water that had to be fifteen or twenty feet deep.

At that same second, Miko hears a shrill police whistle soar above the angry voices behind them. She gives Tim a mind-numbing stare as the three regretfully shoot around the side of a building and rush for the van.

CHAPTER 22

"You heard me right. You have to get out of there!" Tim's throat starts to feel hoarse from tension and the urgency of the words he has propelled into the phone. "They know where Hank lives and could show up any minute. We'll be there real soon, but get everyone ready to go." He glances at Miko as she skids the van around a corner. "I know, I know. But the jazz club is the first place they'll look. Hurry, please."

His ex-partner and ex-girlfriend yanks the steering wheel, just missing a red light while turning onto Granger Boulevard. "Tell them that you lost the piece, idiot." The van roars back in the direction of the sports stadium.

Tim ignores her, concentrating on Jae Kim at the other end of the line. "Yes, we have to bring Hank's wife, too."

"Damn right," the big man agrees, hoping the rest of the team could hear him over Tim's phone.

"I don't know yet where we're going," Tim shouts. "But we're almost to you, so get ready now."

Miko skids into the parking lot beside the jazz club. She intentionally stomps the brake, giving her passengers an extra jar. "I know a place we can hide out," she says with authority, "but you're not going to like it."

⌘

"How's it going?" Tim asks Jae Kim.

The team has gathered at a location near to District 6 where, fifty years earlier, homes had been bulldozed, and families had been driven off by the country's then white-dominated government. At the beginning of the twenty-first century, people finally began moving back into the razed area and so had some of the businesses, both large and small.

Miko hopes that they can go to ground here at one of Birol Kalic's recently-abandoned production warehouses. "To the best of my recollection," she informs the team, "the original sub-assembly of the SpaceZ guidance system was completed here around sixteen months ago."

The dusty offices and manufacturing bays stand empty of aeronautic engineers, equipment fabricators, and other workers, but the basic utilities are still operating, and the abandoned facility is still stocked with cast-off office electronics and leftover construction materials. The only thing lacking, Miko learns, is a good supply of toilet paper.

The team has settled into the site half, feeling safe

from discovery by Hank's uncle and the rest of the BAS. "If they'd figured we're here, we'd've known it by now," says Jae Kim, answering Tim's "How's it going" question.

"That's not what I mean, Doc. I was wondering how your patients are doing."

Jae rubs his forehead as if to clear his thoughts. "I do what I can under these trying conditions, but I can't help feeling it would be better if I were back home with my family. They need me during this crisis. Family is everything."

In Tim's mind, memories flood back of how he left his own family years ago. He struggles to find a worthwhile comment on the subject. "Maybe…if we work together on this, it'll become kind of like family."

Jae gives him a look of utter disgust.

"Okay, maybe not."

Tim notices the subtle change in attitude that is starting to affect his teammates. The accumulated stress is beginning to take its toll. And the fact that no one knows what happened to Boyd is fraying folk's nerves even more. *Pretty soon, the backbiting will start.*

Miko and Jae Kim blame Tim for Louis' injury. Louis and Hank blame each other for not finding the cure. Gicho seems interested in Tim more than he likes, but her brother warns her to forget the idea of such an association. Miko acts guilty or shamed by something. Louis has an unhealthy tendency to doze off too often. And Hank's wife is in increasing pain. Everyone's tempers are on edge.

Arguments have broken out repeatedly until Hank's deep-bass voice draws everyone's attention when he shouts like a drill instructor, "Listen, all of you. None of your little doubts and problems matter. My wife is dying. That's what matters. Hell, my whole race may be dying. And that's only the start. Jae, your concerns for your family are nothing in comparison. Louis, I'm sorry for you, but there's already a cure for *your* pain, and you'll get the full treatment, given time. That's not the case for my wife. Miko, you and Tim have got to stop arguing and get it together, lady. We need big answers, and we need them yesterday. Forget about Boyd. Concentrate on finding the cure. I'll crack some heads, if I have to. Hear me? It's not about right or wrong or justice. It's about saving lives."

Hank's message was clear, but its effectiveness only lasted a short time. Within hours, tempers were rising again, and hope was falling.

Which is why Tim now stands before Jae, steering their conversation back toward the group's current medical issues. "So how's it going with Hank's wife and Louis' head?"

There is a silence, and then Jae sighs, "If we crack the cure, we might save our infected patient." He pauses and consults a printout. "Louis may completely heal, as well. Only time will tell."

"That's good."

"No, that is bad. The one thing we don't have is time. Time to assemble the block. Time to translate the inscription. Time to figure out what the hell the cure is and test it. And in the meantime, women and children continue to expire all over the world."

"It's not as hopeless as all that, is it." Tim hopes he won't get an argument, so he quickly adds, "But we have to at least try and put the pieces together and see what we've got, right?"

Jae fumbles through his pockets, clearly frustrated by failing to find a cigarette. "Assembling the sections of the block into a complete cube will be difficult without the missing piece that you—that fell into the ocean."

"Hey, that's not entirely my fault."

"I know. I know." The Korean slumps and mumbles, "I used to play with puzzles like this one in my youth."

"So, what's this one look like? I haven't seen it since we stole it years ago."

"None of us have, since we split it up." Jae Kim looks up with brimming eyes. "Doesn't all of this seem somewhat ridiculous to you? Running around the world to put together parts of an ancient artifact? Do you seriously think we have a shot at finding a cure?"

Jeez, the Doc's almost a basket case himself. Tim assumes an air of confidence that he isn't sure he actually feels. "It's better than doing nothing." *Smile and shrug.* "Let's just put the pieces together and see if Hank can understand the inscription."

Jae stops searching for a smoke and shows signs of interest again. "We have all but three sections." He clasps his hands behind his back and takes a few paces. "If we ever get yours and Boyd's back, maybe we won't need Hank's."

"Yeah." Tim lets the single syllable draw out. "I

probably should have kept my piece, instead of giving it to the boss. This is not fun."

Jae stops and turns. "No, it's not. This is work."

"And well worth the effort, right? So, don't give up."

"I'm not. I'm not. All right? I just question if we've got enough data to reasonably solve the problem."

"Well, *stop* questioning everything!" Impatience and anger grow in Tim. "We're doing the right thing. I can feel it. We'll find the cure."

"Maybe."

"Fine. Then we'll do it without you." Tim realizes he is clinching his fists and jaw. He wills himself to relax. "I need a drink."

"Or," a clear voice rings out from behind them. "We could all work together and stop acting like guilty losers."

Both men shift their gaze to the other members of their group standing in the doorway behind a tall, lean man. Tim and Kim respond in unison with a single word, "Boyd!"

∽∾∽∾

"So how's it going?" Miko asks, sipping from a steaming mug of Jacobs, South Africa's finest coffee. The strong scented aroma drifts through the lab enclosure where Louis and Jae Kim sit studying the pieces of the Block that rested on a white plastic platform under a strong direct light.

Jae reaches out two fingers of his right hand and delicately rotates the disc to give them all a new perspective.

The markings on the metallic surfaces stand in relief. To Miko, they are totally meaningless.

Louis focuses a mini-camera on the collection of bronze sections and sends the magnified image to a laptop computer.

With a gloved hand, he arranges the pieces horizontally, like a row of oddly-shaped boxcars from a toy train set. "They are all roughly an inch and a half long and a half inch high. Some are L-shaped. One is T-shaped. One is a twisted Z-shape."

Miko takes another sip, holding the mug between her palms. "I can see that."

"They're simple, yet complex in their combination," says Jae. "Now that we have Boyd's and Tim's pieces, we can begin rebuilding the complete cube." He sniffs the air. "Is there any more of that coffee?"

"There's a break room down the hall, past the storage area where I saw Boyd resting on a couple of chairs he's pushed together." She glances in that direction. "He has a host of questions to answer."

"How did he find us, anyway?" Jae asks.

Louis rubs his eyes and temples, as if fighting a strong headache. "I have been sending instant messages to his phone ever since we got to Cape Town. It was Timmy's idea, really. I did not think it would work."

Miko smirks. "Timmy's ideas, as you call them, usually don't, but I'm glad Boyd's all right."

"He looks a little shaky to me," comments Jae.

"I think you're right. Maybe we should start thinking about—" Miko's phone vibrates. She brings it out, sees an unknown number in the display and answers with a cautious, "Yes?"

"Hello, Ms. Wade. My name is Maxwell Hammer. I'm affiliated with Europol as an agent without portfolio."

Weird name. Obviously fake, but intriguing. "Yeah? What are you selling?"

A dry chuckle on the other end of the call. "I'm following up on a lead to locate an escaped prisoner. Boyd."

She can feel the back of her neck stiffening. "Did Birol put you up to this?"

"Birol? No, it's standard security procedure."

Her mind races, but she keeps her voice calm. "Please, don't lecture me on corporate security. I used to run it." She steps away from the two men studying the Block, hoping they won't overhear her conversation.

"Well, you don't any longer," the agent says. "And why is that?"

Miko looks back over her shoulder and sees that Louis and Jae are not listening. "I've stepped down—temporarily. For personal reasons."

"The, let me do my job. Where is Boyd?"

"We don't have time for this sort of—"

"I agree," he hisses. "We don't have time for this. Where is Boyd?"

Her anger flares. *Who the hell does this guy think he is? Is he tracing the call?*

She ends the conversation, blocks the number to avoid call-backs from the jerk and returns to where her two friends sit. She knows she should immediately in-form Boyd of this, but her attention is drawn again to the six little pieces of tarnished metal under the bright light. It looks like they can be put together in more than a hundred different ways to create a blocky tower, a crude chair-shape, or a jagged snake. In each case, the seventh piece leaves a gap in the final construction. "This is hopeless," she says.

"The only reason I am playing with the different configurations," Louis answers, "is that I cannot build the actual block without Hank's missing section."

Miko discovers that she is still holding the mug of lukewarm coffee. She puts it down and bends forward to get a better view of the computer screen. "Can you get close?"

Jae picks up her coffee container and samples a sip. Grimacing, he says, "Sure."

"Show me."

Stacking three of the pieces into a two-inch base, Louis inserts the Z-shaped section into the upper-right corner, followed by the T-shaped part which links into the others from the left. Once all six fragments are in place, there is still a broken opening on the lower left corner where Hank's bit—if they had it—would probably fit nicely.

Kim scratches his left eyebrow in concentration. "Are we sure it was supposed to be assembled into a cube and not some other shape?"

"That's the only shape it's ever been photographed in," says Louis. "It's called the Pandora Block for a reason."

"Yes," Miko muses. "Why Pandora?"

Boyd wanders into the room, messaging a tweak in his shoulder. "She was a mythical woman who opened a box and released all the evil on the world." He still looks a little groggy from the nap Kim had proscribed.

"Yes. I know," Miko answers. "What gets me is that this is a block, not a box."

Boyd replies, matter-of-factly. "I assume that the block does the opposite of the box."

"The opposite, huh? So that's why the block's inscription is supposed to indicate the cure for the virus?"

"We only have Kultar's story for that."

"Kultar?" Louis leans back in his chair and laces his fingers across his chest, thumbs up. "He was your old prison buddy, right?"

Boyd agrees with a sober nod. The last few days of traveling from Korea to South Africa seem to have taken a toll on him. "And he used to be in charge of Birol's collection of art treasures, remember?"

"But he could also be nuts." They turn to see Tim standing in the doorway. He withers slightly under Boyd's firm stare. "Well, someone had to say it."

Miko notices that Gi-cho has followed Tim and now is waiting calmly behind him. *What is it with her?*

"But we still don't have Hank's piece," Jae reminds everyone. "So we can't read the inscription with that gap in the side of the artifact."

Louis says what the rest of the team is already thinking, "Even if Kultar's story is true, we are stumped without the complete block."

Miko squints at the image on the computer screen of the partially-assembled cube. The spiraling stream of etched characters appears to march defiantly along the brazen surface, almost seeming to fall into the chasm where the missing piece belonged. "Maybe not."

"Why?" Kim asks.

Tim and Gi-cho come closer.

Miko stands up straight, massaging her lower back. "We have the photographs."

"Of course." Tim's face beams. "And I'll go you one better."

"What's that?" Boyd asks, stifling a cough.

"Gi-cho found a three-D printer."

"What's that?" Boyd asks.

CHAPTER 23

Louis drops the piece of pale, fabricated plastic into place.

Everyone looks to Hank, who begins writing on a yellow legal pad. "If I'm right, it indicates a mathematical formula of some sort for a, I don't know, frequency?"

Boyd studies Hank's scribbles. "Like a signal or a radio wave?"

"I'll need more time to verify the data," the big man grumbles.

"Can we build something that will generate this frequency?" Boyd searches the faces gathered around him. "You know, like an instrument that'll play the music."

"It isn't music," Hank corrects. "But I'm sure, yes, there's some way we could make this single sound resonate. What are you thinking, bossman?"

Boyd has an astonished look on his face. "I just might know what this is all about."

Miko rests a hand on his forearm. "I'm getting a little tired of your mysterious nature, Jonathan." Her voice is harsh. "We're in too deep now, and you need to tell us the whole story. Just what is your game, anyway?"

Boyd takes a second, seeming to compose himself before answering. "After all these years, I'm not so sure any longer."

⌘

They are still gathered together in the lab—some seated in swivel chairs, some leaning against desks and countertops. Gi-cho sits on the floor, her legs crossed lotus style. The man they all look up to fans a deck of cards, despite the apparent arthritic stab of pain at the base of his right thumb. "It used to be all about righting wrongs and serving justice."

Kim sighs, a little too audibly, but Boyd goes on, spinning one of the cards on the tip of his left index fingertip. "But lately, I've come to realize that what I've really been after is a sense of worth. I want my life to have value in an active manner, if you understand."

"Vaguely," Tim says.

"Justice is important, yes." Boyd inserts the card back into the deck and pauses to rub his stiff and aching shoulder. "But so is self-worth. There are good people in the world and bad. Bad in the sense that they take unfair advantage of others. That shouldn't be the case. So, I guess I'm for fairness."

"A self-appointed referee deciding the play of others in the game of life?"

Boyd shuffles the deck. "Well, when you put it that way…if you see someone taking advantage of someone else, what do you do?"

Louis immediately responds, "Tim would investigate and report it to the public. Miko the same, but with less reporting and more interest in wanting things to turn out right."

"Exactly. And I'm a lot like Miko. I want things to be right, too. But I do more than want. I take steps to ensure that things happen."

"Except, some of your steps go beyond what's right," Hank cautions. "And in that way, you're more like Tim, who always seems to do the wrong thing for the right reason."

"And when he fails, he feels badly and drinks, which is childish," adds Jae Kim.

"Gee, gang," Tim crabs. "With friends like you—"

"I don't know," Miko puts in. "Tim's growing out of his pity-party and boozing phase."

Boyd nods, solemnly. "And that's because he's beginning to see a sense of self-worth. Like me, his's not just after Truth, he's after Redemption. And why, sir, are you making that odd face?"

Tim responds by straightening his expression and stance. "What did you do in your past that drives you to seek redemption? You're guilty of something terrible. Right?"

Boyd puts the cards down on the counter next to

where the pieces of the Pandora Block sit silently displaying their inscription. "You know…I'm not even sure any longer. I don't clearly remember what started it all. It must have been something a long way back in my past, something like the Rosebud slid in that *Citizen Kane* movie."

"So now we're essentially back where we started." Miko shakes her head. "You and you're mysterious nature."

"Maybe you could use therapy," Jae Kim suggests.

"Maybe I could use a drink, doctor."

"I'm for that," Tim got up from his chair.

"All right." Boyd raises his voice. "You want the truth? Here it is."

Tim sat back down.

"I've told some of you about my uncle and his journal." Boyd reaches into the side pocket of his coat and brings out a small red cloth-covered book. "Back in 1947, my uncle Albert was commanding a task force that flew planes out of Ankara, Turkey and over Russian airspace. The US Air Force flew into soviet territory on reconnaissance missions seeking signs of radioactive particles in the air above Stalin's iron curtain as proof that the USSR had detonated an atomic bomb. One of those planes experienced mechanical trouble and when down in the Black Sea."

Tim almost ignores the bottle of beer that Gi-cho has fetched for him. "Go on."

"According to this," Boyd taps the book in his hand, "about a year later, after the crash, the virus struck in a limited way all along the southern and northern shores of the sea."

Hank almost shouts with unqualified interest, "What stopped it?"

"My uncle Albert wasn't sure. The US Government kept the whole outbreak as quiet as possible for national security reasons and to avoid a panic, but his small research group was stumped. The best they could figure, it had something to do with the increased microwaves in the atmosphere due to the growing popularity of television transmissions at the time."

"Microwaves?" Kim reaches over and begins typing on the keyboard of a laptop computer. "That actually rings a bell." Louis slides over to watch the screen.

Miko seems more skeptical than ever. "So you're saying that your uncle caused a bubble of fetid gas from Atlantis to rise up from the middle of the Black Sea and unleash an ancient disease?"

"I never said the word 'fetid.'"

She almost kicks him in the shin, but Tim pulls her slightly off balance. "Actually, that story is almost the same as the one about Birol's SpaceZ fuel tank going down last year in the same location." He starts searching for more information on his phone's web-browser.

"There it is!" shouts Louis.

Jae Kim begins reading from the computer screen. "There was a full scientific report published in a 2015 issue of *Nature*. A group of Chinese researchers used something they called Microwave Resonant Absorption to inactivate a virus. They proposed a reasonable microwave power density that would be safe for use in the open public."

"Look at this." Louis points at the text of the article. "The energy transfer was mainly through physically fracturing the virus structure."

Tim looks up from his mobile. "Television transmissions in the late 1940s were at fourteen-hundred megacycles for the NBC network and seven-thousand megacycles for RCA and NBC. Does that fit?"

Hank looks at Boyd and grumbles, "Sounds like your uncle Albert may have been right about the microwaves vibrating the virus away in 1949. Can we use that now on my wife?"

"I don't know," Jae Kim thinks aloud. "This paper seems to indicate that a pathway toward establishing a new epidemic prevention strategy may exist. Let me see if I can find a methodology to apply the correct frequency."

"But we have the correct frequency," Miko announces, pointing at the cube. "It's right there on the Pandora Block."

∽∾∽

"So how's it going?" Hank asks.

"I wish people would stop asking that." Louis rolls his eyes. He has fed the translated data into a series of the fastest data-processing computers he's cobbled together as a localized distributed network. "I found a patent application for 'a microwave resonant absorption method and device for virus inactivation.'"

"Lemme see." Hank shoulders forward to peer at the PDF of the screen.

The Navajo points to the document's number: *US 2011/0070624 A1*. "It was written by two of the authors of the *Nature* article and contains a rough diagram for a machine that is supposed to generate a beamed frequency that can break apart the helix strands of a nucleic acid of the virus."

"Will it hurt her?"

Jae Kim, who has listened quietly to this exchange, puts a hand up and hums quietly to himself while reading farther into the document. "Says here that the frequency induces a vibration in the virus through MRA without destruction of a water-and-nucleic acid molecule." He locks eyes with the intense Black man. "So, yes, I'd say the method can be applied to human tissue."

"I said, 'will it hurt her?'"

Jae ignores, him but it isn't easy. "We'll have to build a transmitter and test it on something." His eyes drift to look out the window at a grassy area beside the weathered parking lot. Yesterday, he'd seen a small brown animal there, nibbling on a patch of clover.

Hank follows his gaze. "Testing it on a rabbit is dumb. The virus kills human beings, not rodents."

"Let's get the thing built first," Jae reasons. "We should try it out on something simple with a short pregnancy cycle, before we expose your wife."

"Yeah, I guess. But let's hurry, dammit."

☙❧

Calcutta, India:

The aerodynamic design of the Moller M500 Skycar, with its sloping, conical bow, isn't much larger than a Hyundai Elantra, but it is as stable in flight as a much larger aircraft. The four lift nacelles each hold two counter-rotating engines, enabling the vehicle to lift off the ground like a helicopter and move horizontally like a conventional aircraft with a range of over 500 miles.

Birol Kalic steps down from the bright red, two-passenger Skycar that has shuttled him out to the landing platform moored in the Bay of Bengal. The 160-mph craft is his latest toy. It had taken off from the parking lot beside his manufacturing facility outside the city only minutes earlier, to hover over the man-made island where his SpaceZ ships usually land after soaring above the planet's atmosphere.

He pauses for a moment, testing his failing eyesight, before striding purposefully toward the superstructure of the eighty-square-yard platform. His footsteps ring on the carbon-steel deck. Grasping a railing and ascending a steep stairway, he finds Sandrine Lacombe arguing loudly with a man who wears a dark tactical combat uniform.

∽∽∽

Cape Town, South Africa:

Jae Kim's mind is full of doubt. *This is the scariest thing I've ever done.* He watches the woman on the table before him. She lays there panting, her pregnancy having come almost to full term.

Jae has injected some of her infected blood into the rabbit and then performed an autopsy after bathing the animal in the vibrations that emanate from the jury-rigged collection of devices now spread out on a second table next to his human patient. There is a power supply wired to an oscillator connected to an amplifier and isolator which are linked to a directional horn antenna. All the parts have been scavenged from various locations throughout the lab building and were harder to assemble than the Block, itself, even with the help of the patent di-agrams and schematics found on the internet. *In Australia, they'd call this a dog's breakfast.*

As near as he can tell, the test on the rabbit has gone well. The virus within the animal has been shattered suc-cessfully by the handmade Microwave Resonant Absorb-er, but who knows if it will work on Hank's wife. "Are we sure we want to go through with this?"

"We're desperate," Hank reminded him, holding his love one's thin, dark hand.

The equipment hums quietly, ready to be accelerated.

Boyd is the only member of the team who is pacing. The rest stand by, waiting for Jae Kim to gather himself enough courage to put their plan into operation.

This is one frightening operation, the Korean thinks. "I'll say it again: I think this is a bad idea. A hospital would be infinitely better for her treatment. Experiment or not."

"No time," Hank answers. "Move it, Doc."

The woman is in obviously escalating pain. It is her call. She nods grimly, gritting her teeth. "Just get it over with. And don't screw up!"

"I'm *not* an OB-GYN."

"But, you are all we have." Louis is matter-of-fact. "Better get on with it. If this does not work, she will die anyway."

"So will the baby," Tim adds. "We don't have a choice anymore."

Jae fills his lungs as if he were about to dive into deep waters and tries to exude confidence. *This will be the performance of my life. Hers too.*

Louis fingers the dial on the oscillator. "You take care of them, and I will run the machine."

The Korean still hesitates as his sister comes up to stand beside him. "If you do not do it," she whispered, "I shall."

The woman on the table screams.

Miko looks away, biting her lower lip.

Boyd rushes forward to hold the patient in place before the humming device. "We can't wait any longer. The baby's head is crowning."

Jae Kim gives a nod to the Navajo, signaling him to turn the dial. The humming rises in pitch. The modified speaker vibrates on the table. A gush of blood spills from between the woman's cloth-draped legs.

The invisible beam of sound pours from the speaker horn at the end of the jumbled row of equipment.

Jae catches himself praying that the power won't short out or that the city's electrical grid won't fail. *Too damned many things can still go wrong!*

The woman screams again, louder this time.

"Push," Tim yells.

At that moment, Louis moves the dial all the way to the right. The MAR whines and almost shakes itself off the table.

The woman's body shudders. Hank and Boyd hold her firmly in place as if fighting a human hurricane.

Miko reaches her fingers around to bring the baby farther into the world.

Louis clamps both of his arms down on the vibrating pile of equipment, leaning his weight in, while trying to hold the device together and into place.

Hank shouts over the shrieking din. "It's almost here!" His wife's face is a mask of straining fury.

Jae Kim can stand no more. *If it hasn't worked by now, it never will.*

The tiny body slides suddenly into Miko's hands.

Kim comes around to cut the umbilical cord with a pair of scissors he's sterilized with the open flame of his cigarette lighter.

The hum of the equipment lessens, replaced by a new sound—the throaty, full-lunged howl of a newborn boy.

"We did it," Miko gasps. "We beat the bitchin' virus."

Jae is busy checking the mother's pulse. Thready at first, it then settles back to the standard seventy-two beats per minute.

Everyone's attention concentrated on the baby. Except for Hank's. He cradles his wife's head in his arm and kisses her sweat-drenched forehead. "It's a boy, honey. A boy."

"I don't *ever* what to do that again," she gasps in a wavering voice. "Now, let me see him."

As Miko wipes the child clean and presents him proudly to his mother's loving attention, a loud crash rattles through the room.

At first, Jae thinks the MAR has exploded, but then he sees Boyd's prostrate body lying on the floor.

Louis laughs nervously. "The boss just fainted?"

"No," Jae answers, inspecting his fallen friend. "I think it's something else."

CHAPTER 24

Calcutta, India:

Birol has contacted the European Police Office in The Hague, Netherlands, and used his influence to affect Sandrine's release from her incarceration in Paris. Now, the Europol agent assigned, Maxwell Hammer—if that is his real name—stands over six feet tall in his green fatigues and wears his white hair short, almost like a helmet on his bullet head. He seems at ease on Birol's floating platform, looking down his nose and listening to Sandrine rant about Miko's recent underhanded activities.

The French redhead catches sight of Birol's approach and immediately confronts him. "They're after the Pandora Block and plan to meet in Cape Town to assemble it."

He blinks his large eyes at her. It sounds outlandish.

Like something Boyd would come up with as an excuse to distract attention elsewhere. What is the old, bizarre thief actually planning? There is only one way to find out. *And then I can get the sonofabitch back in jail, where he belongs.*

"Mr. Hammer, I've reviewed your CV." Birol draws the attention of the Europol agent. "You've been after Jonathan Boyd for years. Am I correct?"

The tall man turns away from the angered woman and gives Birol a curt nod. "Yes, sir." His burnished-steel eyes didn't blink.

Birol likes that. "Your organization owes me a considerable debt for my past contributions and cooperation."

"I'll bet," Sandrine says boldly.

Birol ignores her and concentrates on instructing Hammer. "I want you to follow up on this assignment and take a tactical team to Cape Town." He glances at Sandrine. "Boyd will undoubtedly be there. You must take him into custody at all costs."

The Europol agent responds crisply. "Yes, sir. We've already been searching for him."

"And report back to me when you locate Miko Wade."

Sandrine claps her hands. "I'll go, too."

"No. You will not. You've caused me enough distraction from our latest launch." He raises his large right hand to indicate the partly-deconstructed rocket that had landed on the platform a week ago. "The next one will be doubly important to one of my financial backers."

"But."

He swings the same open hand around, slapping her sharply across the face.

She goes to her knees with a whimper. Her fingers catch a trickle of blood from a cut on her stunned face.

Birol returns his attention to the Europol man. "Use your full resources to find them."

"Yes, sir."

"Now, go."

Birol looks down at Sandrine Lecombe and pauses to compose himself. He's never been so violent with other women before. Especially, since having the intelligent Miko under him. Pushing back any feelings of remorse, he leaves the redhead and walks along a companionway to his office that overlooks the bay and the city in the distance.

Miko will be back with him soon, he is certain. Her "vacation" will end, and she'll return refreshed and ready to do whatever he demands. His security team is already following up after her, letting her know that he needs her. *Not actually needs, of course. That sounded weak. More like requires her experienced services for a highly personal matter. Yes, that's it.*

She will come to him because he's arranged for her will to favor his direction. She'll solve several nagging concerns, including his interest in locating Jonathan Boyd, late of a Turkish prison.

He will then be able to turn his full attention to the SpaceZ program and its necessary funding. His corporate wealth and position will advance to a level higher than any other businessman outside of the Chinese empire quietly dominating Asia.

ഇരു

Cape Town, South Africa:

"How is it going?" Louis asks in a hushed tone.

Jae Kim has just returned from again checking the woman and child's vital signs. "It looks promising, but we need to wait. I'll run some more tests."

"No, I meant how is Boyd doing?"

Jae sighs, wishing for a cigarette. "There's no way to really tell under these conditions. I have a feeling that he might have somehow reacted negatively to the vibration. I need better equipment and resources than we have here in order to know for sure."

"He seems fine now," Louis offers.

Jae carefully inspects the damage to his friend's injured skull. The bruising has begun to fade. "You don't need that bandage anymore. But, again, I need to check with x-rays."

"It does not hurt."

"You're a terrible liar."

"Not to change the subject, but maybe Miko could talk with Birol Kalic about getting us the resources we need to build a bigger MAR."

Jae finds the crumpled pack in his jacket pocket. The three cigarettes there are mashed and soggy. "A bigger MAR? It would have to be enormous to have any large-scale effect."

"Exactly. Once we find out that the test on Hank's wife was fully successful, we'll need to transmit the frequency on a global scale, blanketing the Earth."

Jae suddenly understands what Louis is thinking. The vastness of his idea is stunning. "Of course—the SpaceZ program."

∽∾∽∾

Calcutta, India:

During a nine-hour flight from South Africa to India, Miko has had plenty of time to organize her thoughts and appeal to Birol for help. She has always thought that he was hiding something from her, but now her returning memories make her suspect him all the more. There is something between him and Boyd that makes her uneasy. *This is the hardest thing I've ever attempted. Perhaps the dangerous, as well.*

Outside the airport, she catches the limo that had been sent from Birol's manufacturing facility and settles back during the drive through the clotted streets.

Her mind begins to wander from the fatigue of the trip. *I'm such an easy mark. I fall for everything. I was taken in by Tim's lunacy years ago, and then again when he turned on the team. I went to Birol after my accident, thinking he would help and eventually found that he was only using me. Now, Boyd has this fantastic idea of finding a cure, and I can't help going along with it by pretending to return to Birol's inner circle, like a faithful puppy.*

The limo swerves to avoid striking a line of school children crossing the intersection, but Miko is so lost in thought that she hardly notices.

I let too many people take advantage of me. I've got to get back in control again, instead of reacting to the wild whims of other people. Unquestionably, Birol has the resources we need to transmit the frequency on a global scale, but I can't stand the idea of letting him manipulate me again.

As the airport limousine delivers her within the massive manufacturing complex, her gut continues to tell her she will want to proceed with caution. Miko is certain that the billionaire will use her return as an opportunity to take command of the situation for his own ends. It will be hard to face the man without flinching. *The hardest thing I've ever attempted.*

She steels herself to tough it out. She will convince him for the sake of her friends and the ultimate cure to the Black Sea Virus. She will risk the chance that he'll try to dominate her, but she is stronger now. She can stand up to him—she hopes.

Entering the security checkpoint at the SpaceZ facility on the banks of the Ganges, Miko finds a beehive of quiet activity. Workers in the various colored uniforms move silently, conversing softly.

She is surprised to find Birol standing in a conference room, conferring with Sandrine Lecombe. The woman is out of jail and wears an organdy blouse and ski pants under an outlandish knee-length fur coat. *God. What miserable fashion sense.*

Miko doesn't let her surprise show outwardly. Instead, she ignores the other woman and goes straight into describing the team's success with the vibration device, attempting to convince Birol that they have found a cure.

The billionaire's smile gradually broadens as he listens to how Hank's wife and child have survived. He looks directly into her eyes and asks, "How can you be sure it will last?"

"We can't."

"But, if you're not certain, you can end the threat, how can—"

"We have to try," she interrupts. "But on a much larger scale. Then perhaps it can be eradicated completely everywhere."

He doesn't seem to like being cut off. But, he is obviously glad to have her back, working for him. One of his large hands comes up and strokes her spine. *Brrr.*

Miko forces a smile. *I can do this.* She moves slightly closer to him. "You—we—can do this."

"I tell you, we can never trust her," Sandrine says coldly. "What Boyd and his team have done is unforgivable."

Miko's voice is equally cool. "You're correct." She runs her tongue along her teeth. "Boyd and his team are children, but they've stumbled into something of worldwide value."

Birol flexes his clasped hands, cracking his knuckles, but makes no other sign to indicate he disbelieves her claim.

Miko requests and receives permission to tend to

personal matters after her long trip. Twenty minutes later, she sits alone in a comfortable office and places a Skype call to Tim. "Have the team pack their equipment and prepare to join me here in Calcutta."

"Are you sure everything will be all right there?" he asks. She gazes at the screen and watches him take a drink from a glass that probably contained straight vodka.

Knowing that the call likely has been monitored, she keeps her comments convincing. "Everything will be fine, I tell you. Except that Sandrine is here. That woman reminds me of cut glass. Hard and beautiful, but easy to see through."

Tim chuckles. "Could be said of you, too, Mik."

She softens the edge on her voice. "For a moment there, you were almost poetic. Then the cynical reporter snapped back into place."

"And I did it all in one sentence, too," he quips.

"Just try and get everyone here in one piece." She ends the call and shakes her head. *He's such a dick.*

☙❧

Cape Town, South Africa:

Boyd's team begins loading the parts of the MAR into Hank's van early the next morning, but no one is in any great hurry. It is the consensus of opinion that this change of venue might be the worst move they can make. What they will gain in resources from working with Birol's SpaceZ program to build a larger version of the microwave transmitter and launch it above the Earth, they can very well loose in the management of those same resources.

Hank makes it known that he intends to stay behind to care for his wife and son. His opinion is firm. "Look at us. A drunken reporter, a gay Navajo, an over-worked Asian and an old thief. What chance have we got against a multi-billionaire and his thousands of worker-ant employees?"

Jae immediately sympathizes with Hank's desire to stay and protect his family, although he resents the "over-worked" label. His thoughts drift back to his own kids and extended family in Busan. He wants to be there with them, instead of traveling to Birol's Calcutta headquarters. *At least I have Gi-cho here with me.*

At first, he had resisted her joining the team, but now she has proven herself to be more than just his little sister. She's grown up considerably in the last few days. He glances to where she stands next to the van, talking to Tim, and wonders how much she *has* grown up.

Boyd is watching the couple as well. Jae catches his eye and strolls over to where the twenty-first century Hood leans against a wooden crate. "Sometimes I can't believe how far the world has gone out of whack since the old days."

Boyd fumbles out a pack of cigarettes and jerks one partly out for Jae to accept. The two men light up and share a moment. "Only six or seven years ago, we all had hope for the future," Boyd mutters. "We thought we could solve the world's problems, heal the sick, feed the hungry and educate the poor." He blows out a plume of gray smoke. "Now, all that's been pushed aside, first by the virus and then by its after effects of panic and fear."

Jae grunts, looking at the weeds and gravel in the eroding parking lot. "Life has become a series of deadly challenges. Everyone is justifiably out for themselves." He decides to try and lighten the mood. "You know, I remember how you used to grit your teeth, crack a molar and spit it into the face of evil."

"I was never that strong," Boyd smirks, stepping on the butt of his cigarette. "And at my age, I should probably give up smoking those things, or I'll fall completely apart."

"Hey, now. As your doctor, I can pronounce you fit and strong. You're just not as young as you used to be, if you know what I mean."

"And you, my friend…" Boyd lets the rest of his words drift into the morning breeze. He raises his head and gazes out to the far end of the parking lot. "We've got company."

As the final sections of the crated MAR are being stacked into the van, a silver SUV pulls up. Before anyone can react, a tall man in fatigues and white hair gets out and comes toward them.

"I'm Maxwell Hammer of Europol." He holds up a black ID wallet. "I'm here to take Mr. Boyd into custody."

CHAPTER 25

Tim recognizes Hammer from past reports he has read of Europol in the press. Years earlier, the law enforcement agency had benefited from the information acquired and shared from Boyd's early operations. The info exposed detailed secrets of organized crime throughout the Mediterranean and the European agency was more than glad to get it.

The most recent reports Tim read a few months back indicated that Europol shifted its focus to investigating, countering and disrupting terrorism and cybercrime among the fourteen nations of the European Union. Ironically, one of the member nations is Turkey.

It seems strange for the organization to show up here today in South Africa, interested in recovering an escaped prisoner like Boyd.

Tim confronts Agent Hammer. "As I recall, you have no authority in this country."

"We'll settle that later," the Europol man says, drawing his sidearm. "Now, hand him over."

Boyd remains calm, raising his hands in surrender.

Tim sees three bright red dots appear on Boyd's chest. *The supercops must've stationed snipers on top of buildings throughout the abandoned industrial park.*

"This is a mistake," Louis warns.

"We don't want any trouble," Tim adds. "We're on our way to join Birol Kalic's operation in India."

At first, Hammer appears mildly confused by this comment.

Tim detects a note of concern in the agent's features and stance. But the red laser specks don't waver from Boyd's body.

"Like I said," the tall operative drawls, studying the team, "he's coming with us."

Gi-cho steps in front of Boyd. The ruby spots now cover her lean chest.

Hammer sputters. "What are you—get back!"

Her brother comes forward to protect her. Jae stands before his sister without a word, glaring at the agent and blocking the dots that now slightly wobbled on his frame. "This ends now," the Korean announces.

Confusion works its way across Hammer's face. He starts to push at Jae to move him out of the line of fire.

Tim joins his team members and finds one of the red points of light dancing on his own chest. *Jeez!*

"Stop it," Hammer spits.

Louis nearly stumbles to add his body to the line of protesters. "I stand with Timmy."

"Thanks, Featherstone," Tim grins, feeling his knees tremble.

The Europol agent grimaces and swears in a language that Tim does not understand. But the meaning is clear to all. Using his shoulders to shove the group aside, Hammer forces his way past and brings the barrel of his weapon up in the ultimate threat. But Boyd is gone.

The gang spreads out, indicating that they are harmless.

Europol agents swarm the area, searching, while Tim calls Miko on his mobile.

Within minutes, she contacts Birol, who comes on line and confirms publically that the team is approved to travel with their equipment to India.

Hammer and his men take their time grousing and searching the area again and finally the van, before allowing the group to leave.

Standing in the entrance of the manufacturing building where his wife and new-born son wait, Hank waves goodbye to them all.

കൗന

Calcutta, India:

Miko Wade stands inside the superstructure of the giant platform barge in the Bay of Bengal, closer to the Tropic of Cancer and at a latitude more southern than Cape Canaveral. A mild breeze comes off the water's surface. She holds back a few random strands of hair that tickle her face and stares back at the shore, and the tip of the two-stage rocket pointed into the clear azure sky. The modified SpaceZ ship's elegant, streamlined design is disrupted by the ugly, dark bubble of the large-scale MAR attached to its upper stage. She shakes her head ruefully. *How about that? Damned thing looks like it's pregnant.*

In a way, she is right, because if all goes as planned, the rocket will launch and give birth to a sound that will bring life to thousands of suffering virus victims. No existing satellite already in orbit is designed to transmit the required frequency to resonate a vibration strong enough to shatter the Black Sea Virus. If successful, Miko and the others will have applied their combined skills and knowledge, believing that this launch might well represent mankind's only chance for stopping the BSV before it mutates.

The rapid configuration and complex assembling effort have exhausted everyone, especially Louis, who collapsed only an hour ago and has been transported to an infirmary for treatment of his lingering head wound. Working intently with Jae Kim he has overseen the construction of the rocket's black bulge and its contents during the last week. Russian aeronautic engineers in Birol's employ have followed their directions and worked feverishly to fabricate the device and attach it to the space-going vessel.

Miko finishes a mind-numbing eighteen-hour shift. She forced herself to concentrate and manage two separate teams of technicians as they made final preparations for tomorrow's launch. She has seen little of Tim, but hears that he has successfully arranged logistics for all the necessary equipment and components to be assembled during a grueling schedule. *I really didn't think he had it in him.*

Sandrine, on the other hand, has taken on the easy job of coordinating the media for the event, conferring almost hourly with Birol. *That used to be my job, but she's welcome to it. Keeps the asshole away from me.*

The woman has wormed her way into conducting a series of interviews with government officials and members of the press.

Birol is already beginning to take credit for stopping a world-wide epidemic and reminding everyone that the "Z" in SpaceZ originated from his middle name, Zeheb. *We haven't even launched yet, and he's crowing about his great success.*

Miko is surprised how strongly she desires to spend the final night with Tim, but Gi-cho is never far from him. The slim Korean woman is obviously smitten and, almost in revenge, Miko's thoughts drift away, remembering the classic, cool demeanor of Jonathan Boyd. *Where has he gotten to during these last furious days?*

An international team of medical researchers has analyzed and verified the curative effects of the MAR's frequency vibrations. They conclude that while the cure works in individual applications, such as it had with Hank's wife, there is no way to know for certain if it will be equally successful on a large scale when the microwaves are transmitted from the upper atmosphere.

And there is no time to conduct additional proto-type tests.

The news each day is full of the growing toll the virus is taking on the Black race. Some religions now claim that the deaths are an act of God. Groups like the KKK rejoice in the seemingly justified confirmation of their racist beliefs. Panic, riots and even small wars break out as the first reports begin to circulate that the virus has started to affect Indonesians and women of Mongol descent. World-wide financial markets start to crumble. The word 'extinction' appears for the first time in the press, followed by twitter feeds and trembling lips.

Miko is not immune to the fear. She struggles to remain calm and focused on the gigantic task at hand.

On the evening before the launch, after all processes and sub-routines have been triple-checked, she finds herself yearning again for the company of Tim Cross. Birol has been demanding her attention, but she desperately wants to regress to another simpler time when her life seemed much less chaotic.

She isn't a bit surprised to find him in a bar down the highway from Birol's manufacturing facility. He sits alone on a stool with a large can of Fosters in his hand.

She slides into the space beside him. "Remember the time we got back those stolen Van Goghs from the Italian mafia?"

He turns and arches a reddish eyebrow. "Shh. They still don't know."

Funny. She toys with an ashtray, careful not to return his gaze. "It was my favorite heist."

Tim takes a slug from his can of beer. "Ah, the good old days."

She decides to try and share her feelings. Clearing her throat, she takes the plunge and says, "I'm stuck."

"Eh? Sorry. Long day." He swallows another swig. "You were saying?"

He's not making this easy. She waves the bartender away and goes on with on with her, what? Confession? "I'm stuck in a place I—"

"A place where you don't belong, Mik?"

She huffs, "I was going to say—"

"What?"

Miko blinks at him, uncertain if he's sober. "What, what?"

Sighing, Tim says, "What do you want?"

"Why?"

"I'm an investigator." He chuckles. "I want to know things, that's all."

Miko feels her temper rise. "You're a coward, and all you ever want is to drink."

He turns away. "I can't talk to you."

"Fine," she says, which it isn't. "I can't either." *So there.* She leaves him just as she had found him—alone and staring into the mirror at the back of the bar.

It has not gone anything like want she'd planned. Miko spends the rest of the night in constant waves of fury and tears, at last falling into a troubled sleep around three a.m.

⟡⟡⟡

Everywhere:

Mutate, grow, spawn, reassemble. Tissue bends, re-forms to push out, seeking to grow again. Mindlessly driven to expand. Compelled to dominate and convert all it can to a half-life of biological de-formation. Pulse, swell, pulse, invade.

∾

Bay of Bengal:

Bright and early in the morning, Miko again climbs the metal ladder to stand on the platform out in the bay. A crowd of more than one hundred workers and technicians not involved in the launch wait expectantly. All eyes watch for the slightest sign of movement back on shore where the SpaceZ ship stands on its fortified concrete pad, slim and tall, like a 230-foot pencil standing upright on its eraser.

A collection of yachts, junks, speedboats, and even a mid-sized cruise ship floats near the platform. Spectators and well-wishers from a variety of countries gaze with hope as the countdown begins.

Approximately thirty-five seconds before ignition, the umbilical cord with its external power and cooling lines drop. Miko can detect the tone of excitement in the voices coming from the hand-held video phones. The automatic ignition switches on and the engines light up in a glare. The boosters start to roar as the engines build up to their proper thrust. Then the massive hold-down clamps fall away.

Within the blinding flare of fire, more than 30,000 gallons of water per second gush forth to quench the flames and protect the skin of the machine. Massive, man-made clouds of steam explode into the air above the pad.

The launch is sluggish at first, like an elevator rising to the sky. The lift-off is gradual and smooth. The thin ship rejects the earth with a flawless effort, her flame spurting backward white-hot, changing rapidly to a brilliant yellow ball of fire, and a streamer of barely-visible shock waves from behind.

There is nothing violent about it. *Nice and easy.* She lifts straight up, her flame lashing the air behind her, accelerating steadily, smoothly, rapidly.

Miko's heart beats furiously in her chest. She catches herself humming to the sound of the engines. Without thinking, she shouts with joy, "Go, baby, go!"

The people around her, including Tim and Gi-cho, are craning their heads, gesturing their hands and jabbering away in more half-a-dozen languages. The excitement is contagious. In less than a half-minute after take-off, Miko senses a hot trembling in the air from the launch area. It blows across her entire body and into her chest. *The most amazing thing I've ever seen.*

The rocket continues to roar, climbing to 35,000 feet and encountering the highest aerodynamic forces from a combination of increasing acceleration and thinning atmosphere. Miko squints through binoculars. *Did the ship just shudder?* She reminds herself that it is only the haze from the heat of the engines.

An object thrown into space can go into orbit at a rather low altitude, say one hundred miles up. This one does not need to stay up for years. In fact, the world will know within days if the MAR has the desired effect. So, the SpaceZ launch only needs to top out at 10,000 miles at a little over 16,000 mph.

The crowd on the platform watches the pencil-line of white trail marking the ship's ascent until the fiery point in the sky dwindles into nothingness. Now comes the long wait. Miko worries about the unknown. *There were so many things that we could have gotten wrong.*

Hank's distraught translation. Kim's untested medical knowledge. Louis' decoding skills, possibly hampered by his head wound.

We're all in uncharted territory and won't know the results of the orbiting MAR for at least twenty-four hours.

During the uncomfortable pause following the launch, several members of the team fill the time by checking in on the Louis Nakai at the medical center. The Navajo lies quietly in a hospital wardroom, uninformed to the day's events, but the doctors say his injury requires only a minor operation to relieve the pressure on his right-frontal lobe.

Miko stays with him the longest and is the one to see him briefly come awake when a nurse checks his vitals. He smiles once at Miko and sips some water from a straw that she holds for him. "We did it, Louis. The frequency resonator is up there beaming down the wavelengths we interpreted from the Pandora Block."

"The block—" he repeats, his eyes starting to droop.

"You're going to be all right," she urges, seeing that he is again falling into slumber.

"The block," he mumbles again. "Why?"

"Just rest, Louis."

"Why—was the block—separated—into pieces?"

CHAPTER 26

Only I have been successful in saving everyone." Birol Kalic sits back in the seat of his limo as it speeds through the crowded streets of Calcutta. Outside, the Howrah Railway Station flashes past, as the climate-controlled car pulls into Chowringhee Road on its way to the United Bank of India. He has a CNN video-interview scheduled to take place there in twenty minutes.

The limousine's horn blares above the surrounding shouts and bicycle bells to create a wall of noise. A flotilla of motorbikes, rickshaws, and bullock carts vie for the narrow lane of pot-holed pavement. Banners hang from electric wires that span the street filled with the unceasing flow of brown-skinned humanity. A wide-belted police-man holds up traffic long enough to let the limo pass.

Birol notes the body of a decomposing pregnant woman lying face up in the gutter. *These people are so expendable here. The cost of labor is so low.* The glazed decaying eyes protrude. He puts a hand up to block the view and forces down a shiver.

"You can use this successful launch," Sandrine Lecombe assures him, "in so many ways. The world will finally see you for the great man that you are. We need to be out in front on this."

The woman's eagerness begins to play on his nerves. He swivels his head away from her and swipes left to view another financial report on his tablet. The numbers are not good. In fact, they are the worst in his many years of corporate life maneuvering.

The Chinese funding has failed to be approved. The cartel has not let it go through. They backed away from his proposals, partly due to the intensifying world crisis and partly due to the disclosure of his holdings in other significant Asian countries, including the missile testing operations here in India.

His accounts are starting to dwindle. Soon he will have to fall back on his financial nest egg, the collection of priceless art hidden in his vaults. But so much of his international dealings have changed and shifted with the unpredictable unrest fomented by the virus. He doesn't know any longer if there is a viable market for either his European paintings or Oriental treasures. He gives an uneasy laugh. *I could be broke already and not know it.*

Birol lets his thoughts drift to the Mona Lisa sketch that Sandrine has brought him. He shakes his head with wistful doubt and resolves to forget such trinkets. Right now, he needs to bring his full attention to attaining a position in the eyes of the world that will allow him to dominate with authority.

He knows that the universal acclaim he's received from launching the latest SpaceZ with its intricate frequency device will be fleeting. His best chance of cashing in on this new notoriety is to double-down with the Russian Council. They *will* support him and possibly fund him through this financial crisis. He might even have a shot at becoming a major player within their organization. Yes, he would gladly sacrifice his cache of art holdings under those conditions, in order to gain such a high level of power in this decaying geo-political environment.

Suddenly satisfied, the billionaire pours himself a glass of water from the limo's mini-bar, but offered none to Sandrine. Instead, he leans forward and demands of the driver, "Can we move this along?"

Fifteen minutes later, as scheduled, he is speaking before a sea of video cameras and microphones. He forms his statements with solid confidence. "Pompous and ignorant businessmen started this vicious form of biological warfare, and the populace needs to bring them to task, to trial, and to take away their resources, so they can never again prey on the defenseless public."

A roar of applause rolls up from the crowd. His name begins to come back to him in a rhythmic chant. So much so that he cannot go on with the rest of his speech. His words are drowned out, to his very great pleasure. He waves, bows, nods, points, and, still, they do not stop cheering. Finally, he gives a last opened-handed salute to them all and leaves the stage from a back entrance.

Sandrine adjusts the microphones as the crowd quiets. "Mr. Kalic is an idealist. He believes in justice and fairness throughout the world."

Climbing back into his limo, Birol hears the crowd roar again in a satisfying and idiotic response to her ringing words.

⁊つ⁊つ

Everywhere:

The faint resonance grows. Pulse, snap, pulse, shatter. Silent death. One section breaks off. Another vibrates and falls away. Neighboring tissue absorbs the liberated protein. Growth dwindles. Too much energy soaks in. Counter-vibrations fight the impulse to expand. Processes speed up randomly until a critical state is reached. The fabric of the virus tears apart, dissolves—is destroyed silently, precisely, completely.

⁊つ⁊つ

Calcutta, India:

Miko sighs. "We need to talk."

"If it's about us, I'm interested," Tim says.

"There is no 'us,'" Miko answers. "It's about Louis."

"Oh, God, is he okay?"

They are Skyping—Miko from her modest hotel room, Tim in some bar again where the lighting is dim.

"He's…better," she says unevenly. "But he's mumbling about the Block and asking why it was broken."

"I wondered about that too, actually." Tim's face smears suddenly as he repositions the camera on his phone. "Maybe we all did, but we had too much on our plates to stop and consider it."

She waits for the image to settle down. *God, the lines of communication are breaking down.* "Have you noticed the increased reports of minor earthquakes?"

He yawns. "You mean the one in northern Alaska and the volcanic activity in Hawaii? Wait. Are you saying that someone is attacking the United States?"

"No, of course not." She breathes deeply to calm herself. "The US just happens to have the most sophisticated sensing equipment and the fastest method of electronically reporting the news. I've done some further checking, and minor shocks are starting to occur in other parts of the world." She immediately reads the skepticism in his expression, but hurries on. "If you look at the timeline over the last two days, you'll find that the increased incident of tremblers began only a few hours after we sent up the MAR."

At first, he stammers as her words sink in and the idea takes hold. "My God! *We're* the cause. It's a side effect of the vibrations."

"That's what I'm beginning to think."

He rubs a hand over his eyes. "It must be causing a geological resonance as the satellite flies in low-earth orbit around the continents."

Miko nods. "And that's why Louis is babbling about

breaking up the Block. The ancients who constructed it knew that the frequency would shatter the virus, but then they must have discovered that the vibrations also initiated a shifting of the ground beneath their feet."

"And that's why they broke into sections," Tim surmises. "To keep the cure hidden, because it turned out to be a greater danger than the disease."

"You know what this means?"

"That old guy, Kultar, was right? And Atlantis was real?"

"They were destroyed by their own cure."

"Holy crap," he responds, almost too dramatically. "The quakes must have caused their island civilization to sink into the…the depths of the Black Sea."

"I'm serious, dammit," says Miko. "We've got to stop the signal broadcasting from the MAR before it gets some other land, like maybe in Hawaii or the Caribbean, goes under."

"Or the San Andreus fault splits open." This time he sounds sincere. "It'll take parts of California into the Pacific."

At that moment, a small window opens on the screens of both their devices. Tim almost drops his phone. Miko looks down at the text window and sees that a call is coming in from *RECALLEDTOLIFE*.

She frowns and taps the Facetime icon. "Where the hell are you?" she shouts when Boyd's face comes on the screen. There are deep lines running from beneath his eyes to the corners of his mouth. He looks leaner than before, and his eyebrows are now silver-gray. His voice is patient. "I hear that the launch was a complete suc-cess," he says in greeting. "And that a great number of births are starting to occur. How is Louis?"

Tim echoes Miko's question. "Where the *hell* are you?"

After a pause, Boyd answers, "I'm on a modified cruise vessel out in the middle of the bay. You may have noticed the ship when you were in Cape Town. It's the one I mentioned when we were in St. Thomas."

Miko remembers seeing a small cruise ship floating near Birol's platform during the launch. "So that's how you got out of Busan. You had a special boat or yacht off the coast of Korea."

"It's a carryover from my early days and the only way I've been able to avoid pursuit."

Tim's face in the Skype screen stares at Miko. "See? I told you. He's a pirate."

She almost throws the phone to the floor of her hotel room.

"Listen, kids," Boyd's voice holds a persuasive tone, "I've been with you here at sea, ready to help, if needed, the entire time."

"That's bullshit," Miko counters. "You've been hid-ing, while we did all the heavy lifting."

The image of Tim blurs slightly as he leans into the camera. "No. Look at him. I talked with Jae Kim about Boyd's condition. He has a modified form of the BSV. Am I right?"

"Believe me," says Boyd. "I knew when we started, that my uncle and other members of my family had contracted a dormant version of the disease back in the 1950s. It mutated our DNA and slowly took the lives of my mother and others over the last decades."

Tim nods while he speaks. "According to Jae, you knew you would be next, and that's why you reacted so terribly when we ran the test on Hank's wife."

"Yes, I had no idea that the test would cause such an accelerated reaction within my cells. There may not be a cure for my version of the virus, but at least we saved the world."

"That's what you think," Miko says. "We need to get the team back together again. And fast"

❧❦❧

Even after the SpaceZ satellite stops transmitting the virus-killing signal, the quakes continue and intensify. The harmonics resonate along seduction zones causing tectonic plates to shift and rise through the earth's mantle. Seismic disturbances occur at boundaries that have been inactive for thousands of years.

The Caribbean plate shifts, swamping both St. Thomas and St. Croix. The Eurasian plate butts into the Indian plate, causing destruction near Calcutta.

The Ring of Fire in the Pacific Ocean crumbles parts of Los Angeles and San Francisco.

The long cloud-spewing chain of volcanos along the western shore of South America light up the night sky with fiery death.

Every race of Man is now in danger.

New riots and chaos strain the world's resources. Governments are on the breaking point. The Russian military takes possession of great tracts of land and vast populations beaten down by the on-going effects of the quakes.

Birol and the people around him are protected from the invading Russian forces, leaving Miko and the rest of the team safe to focus on ending the new earth-shattering threat.

The fact that they are the core cause, for good reason or not, propel them to seek a solution. Their knowledge and experience with the MAR and its frequency give them hope for a chance to find a way to control it all.

"We need to do more than just turn off the transmitter up in the SpaceZ," declares Miko.

Tim agrees. "We need a counter vibration that will dampen and possibly mute the effects of the MAR."

"Something like white noise that will block the frequency," Jae considers. "And we need it transmitted again worldwide."

Tim urges the team on. "But we can't just reprogram the MAR from down here on Earth."

Louis has recovered enough to join the team briefly at Birol's industrial complex. His head is still bandaged from the operation that relieved the pressure on his brain, but his mind and spirit are as quick as ever. "Then let us build another one and send it up in another SpaceZ to broadcast the counter—what is wrong?"

Miko's voice is flat. "There is no other SpaceZ ship available, and, besides, I'm not sure Birol would agree.

He's set himself up within the Russian Counsel as a key member gaining power from all the chaos."

"Then we've created a monster?"

Jae looks at Tim. "More like a world dictator."

"Let me talk with him," Miko says.

CHAPTER 27

Saturday, August 1, 2020:

There is no talking to Birol. He absolutely refuses to consider the proposal.

Since the billionaire will not support their cause and instead takes advantage and credit for the results, the team decides to transfer operations to Boyd's vessel in the bay.

The superyacht sports a lounge on the sun deck with full bar and Jacuzzi and a solon on the bridge deck that converts into a cinema. The heart of the vessel is its circular-inlaid marble floor in the center of the atrium. Steps away are two exquisite etched-glass staircases that draw the eye upward to a cascading crystal chandelier.

But now that the team's research equipment and Louis's network of computers have been installed, the wide-beamed compartment looks like a cross between a video studio and an astronomy lab. A huge monitor tree is set up where the Navajo and other members of the team work together to establish communications with major television and internet news outlets.

"This boat is incredible!" Tim comments, looking in the direction of the bar.

"It used to be a double-hulled exploration ship that sailed between Tierra del Fuego and the Ross Shelf," Boyd says with genuine pride. "She's fifty-four meters long and sleeps twelve. Flying two flags under a unique dual registration in the UK and Cayman Islands, its twin Caterpillar diesel engines provide thirty-seven-hundred horsepower for a cruising speed of seventeen knots."

"Uh-huh," Tim replies.

Boyd pauses. "What are you searching through your pockets for?"

"I could have sworn I had a gun here somewhere." The reporter grins.

"Oh, fine. Now I understand why Miko thinks you're such a clown." Boyd recovers his composure. "Anyway, I had parts of the ship's hull converted to create this luxury cruise liner, back before we all met."

"I sometimes forget that that you had a life before the turn of the century."

"There's a lot about him that you don't know," a broad-shouldered man with platinum hair speaks, coming out of a companionway.

Tim almost chokes. "What the *hell* is Hammer doing here?"

"I'm sorry," Boyd quickly responds. "I'd hoped to

explain his presence before you found him here."

The reporter automatically looks down to check his chest for any red laser rifle dots. Exhilaration runs through him. His muscles stiffen for fight or flight.

Boyd gives a hardy laugh. "Don't worry about Joseph, here." He drapes an arm around the Europol agent's shoulders. "He and I have been friends for years."

Hammer smiles. "Although Birol Kalic doesn't know it."

"Son-of-a—I get it," says Tim. "You're undercover for Boyd." He quickly switches the tone of his voice. "So is your name *really* Joseph, or what?"

"No. And it's not Maxwell Hammer either." The platinum-haired man relaxes and finds a seat on a curved sofa as if the yacht were his home away from home.

Tim studies Boyd, carefully. "Where do you dig up these phony names, like Jonathan Doe Boyd, anyway?"

The master thief coughs mildly, as if to clear his throat. "When I was a boy, I would have said from a box of Crackerjacks."

Hammer's thick accent wraps itself around a question. "What is Crackerjacks? Explosives maybe?"

Tim runs his fingers through his ginger hair and glances in Hammer's direction, "Never mind. But when we have a moment free, you have *got* to tell me all about the boss's background."

Hammer's eyebrows go up. "You call him boss? He's only lucky. He gambles too much. Thinks he has a gift for winning at cards, but it's only bullheadedness."

"And you," Boyd presses a hand against Hammer's

shoulder, "are an unordinary man with unordinary af-
fairs."

"What does that mean?" Tim ventures.

The Europol man gives a pained expression that suggests Boyd has said a bit too much. "I'll tell you later."

⅌⅌⅌

Jae Kim stands in the small cabin on the second deck
of the yacht and sorts through the boxes of medical sup-
plies he's had brought on board. Having finished studying the latest readouts of Louis Nakai's injury, he finds
himself in a hopeful mood. *The worst has passed. At least
for my friend.*

Gi-cho comes down the passageway to stand next to
her brother. She gently taps his elbow. "Tell me more
about Mr. Cross, please."

Jae notices the faint indent between her eyes that he
likes to call her "I want" line. He doesn't think she knows
that it gives away her feigned composure. "Tim?" He returns his attention to the reports in his hand. "Why do you
ask, mouse?"

She snatches up a white roll of adhesive tape, picking at its edge with a fingertip. "He interests me. Slightly."

"Let me guess. Now, you find *him* complex and mysterious. You must get your hormones under control."

Before she can reply, Boyd passes by the hatch and
informs them that Miko is arriving back in the launch.
"Everyone should come topside for the news."

Jae climbs the ladder with his sister. He can just make out the small boat motoring in from the shore. It will come alongside in minutes.

"I think your ship is beautiful," Gi-cho mentions casually to Boyd. She runs her slim hand along the smooth brass railing. Sunlight gleams off the polished teakwood and her ink-dark hair. "I could live here forever."

Between the sight of the brass bright-work and the crystalline-glass windows facing the calm blue water, Jae experiences a moment of peace, as if he were all drifting in a fairyland. "I must admit that this boat is truly dream-like."

Boyd shares his thanks with the young woman. "The ballast and bulk of the ship hold it level and steady in the mild sea breeze that skims across the bay. She was built in the mid-eighties and can cruise at a fair-the- well clip in good weather, like this."

Jae listens with half attention. Despite the general moment of calm conversation, the ravishing effects of the virus are never far from his thoughts, but it was oddly refreshing to hear Boyd talk about something he clearly enjoys.

"She can sleep twelve with comfort. More, if we pack them in two to a cabin, but when we're at full capacity, it puts a strain on the galley and our fresh water reserves."

"Oh, the crew wouldn't like that, I'm sure," Gi-cho says. "How did she get her name?"

Boyd smiles and strokes his hand along a rope-entwined stanchion. "She's French-made from the ship-yards in Nice, which explains the name, *La Derniere Dalphine*."

"*The Last Princess*," Jae bobs his head, looking sideways at Boyd. "You're always a romantic."

The tall man ignores the complement. Instead, he gazes over Jae's shoulder. "Ah, here comes Miko. Let's hope her news is good."

℘℘℘

"Birol won't cooperate. That bitch, Sandrine, has his ear, and he refuses to listen to reason. I'm not even sure he still has enough resources any longer to build a second SpaceZ rocket."

"So we're screwed, huh?" asks Tim. "The tremblers will continue and the world will fall apart."

They sit together in the main lounge, dejection in their voices.

"Or we wait," Miko says, "and hope that the quakes settle down, and Birol picks up the pieces, taking full command of almost everything."

Tim rubs his temples. "And it's all on us." Bitterness fills his tone. "It's our own fault, because we stopped the virus and helped put him out in front of the world as a leader with the cure."

"But we're the ones who started the frequency vibrations that are shaking the world apart," responds Jae.

Louis grimaces. "Then we should be the ones to stop the vibrations."

"How?" Tim insists. "We don't have a ship to broadcast a counter-frequency that will cancel the effects of the original signal."

"Why do we need a ship?" Boyd says.

Tim continues his train of thought, feeling more miserable and helpless than ever. "The government can send up a missile and destroy the satellite, but we need another ship to send out the new frequency."

"Again," Boyd asks, "why do we need a ship?"

"He's right, you know," the Navajo thinks out loud. "All we really need is another way to conduct a worldwide broadcast of the counter-frequency. Something like a huge live-streaming conversation cast out over the internet."

"That's it!" Miko looks at Louis, her eyes alight with inspiration. "An enormous on-line flash mob event!"

 споь

They have a plan now. The only problem is to find a way to execute it with enough sonic volume and force strong enough to counteract the vibrations. If their previous activity in creating the MAR and launching it into orbit was feverish, this new plan to counter the frequency was even more intense. It has to move forward at a frenzied pace. Fortunately, they do not have to build or launch anything physical this time. All they need do is use their positions and contacts in the media to persuade urgent cooperation to get the message out.

"Yes, that's all," Miko thinks. *A billion-to-one shot!*

CHAPTER 28

Yes, I understand the concept of a counter resonance to nullify the original signal." Agent Hammer of Europol winces in thought. "I just don't see how we can make it big enough to do any good."

A new quake shakes the area, inducing instant panic. The yacht wobbles in the resulting waves. Most of the troupe of ex-thieves tries to remain calm while brainstorming in the ship's lounge area. Boyd lies in a bunk below recovering from a severe coughing fit he'd rather they not know about.

"Look. It's easy…I think," Miko explains. "All we have to do is get enough people to broadcast the new sound into the atmosphere. They can turn up the volume on their mobile phones at a specific time and add their transmission to the television and radio broadcasts."

"I've seen it done at sporting events," Tim adds. "An

entire stadium of people hold their phones up high to shine a light down on the field. It's like doing the Wave, but with electronics."

"But what television and radio broadcasts?" Their eyes are drawn to the CNN broadcast that pans across a Japanese shoreline were a nuclear power station is crumbling into the sea. "Jesus, we're so screwed. These newscasts look like the end of the world."

"No. That's a good thing." Louis holds one side of his injured head.

"*What*?" Tim almost spills his drink.

"Remember what Boyd said about how the virus was snuffed out in the early 1950s by the sudden increase of microwaves coming from all the new TV stations?" the Navajo reasons.

"Oh, I get it!" Hammer's deep voice fills the lounge. "We contact the media and have them send the counter signal into the sky, and the original transmission will be cancelled out."

"Only in areas where TV transmission is strong enough. But there are still parts of the world where we need people to augment the signal, using their phones."

Tim says what they are all thinking. "This is a big challenge. How do we get people on board?"

"We should start by sending out a text message." Louis's eyes have a distant look in them. "We will carefully urge the media to tell people to transmit the tone at a precise point in time, say, one p.m. GMT."

"That's a tall order," Miko says sharply. "How can we get people to cooperate and know what to do?"

Louis seems to be speaking to the sky. "Tim, you have contacts with the press. Miko, you know major leaders in several countries. Hammer can help spread the word with his contacts in Europol. Boyd—"

"That's a good point. What will the counter frequency do to Boyd?" Hammer asks.

"There's…no telling," Jae admits, weakly, "but we've got to try."

Tim sets his drink down. "I think it's our only hope."

☙☙

Later that afternoon, Miko finds Boyd at the fantail, breathing in the cool sea air.

"I think you know this already," she comments, "but I need to say it. When Tim turned on you, I left him."

"I didn't want that to happen," Boyd mutters, staring into the open ocean.

"What makes you think you can play with people's lives?"

The question must have caught him off guard, which is what she'd intended. He clears his throat. "You two were like the son and daughter I never had."

"I was like a daughter to you?" She bristles. *Okay, breathing back to normal. Almost.* "I was afraid you thought that."

Boyd covers his mouth. A racking cough comes from deep in his chest. "Excuse me. Caught a cold and can't seem to shake it."

She sees the tears growing at the edges of his eyes. "Has Jae Kim checked that out?"

Boyd rubs his lips with the back of his long-fingered hand. "We have a deal." He winks. "I don't bother him, and he doesn't bother me."

"You sound like my Grandpa Stanley. He hates doctors, too."

"Indeed," the elder thief answers. He pauses, as if unsure what to say. A gull swoops past. Then he adds, "I think Tim has the best cure—a couple shots of Wild Turkey." He looks at her with a penetrating gaze. "You and he really should get along better, you know."

It dawns on Miko that Jonathan Boyd has never shown any real interest in her as a woman. *And my feelings for him have been like a school-girl crush.*

Without taking a step, she slowly moves away from him.

☙☙☙

"If you want the honest truth—" Miko takes a breath. "—it broke my heart when we had to separate."

Slightly stung by her words, Tim looks down. He knows that she had called him here to her cabin in order to set the record straight. The tone of her voice tells him that. And he knows that it is time for them to clear the deck, so to speak. "I thought," he tries to confess, "that I was protecting us."

"Stop being so goofy and dopey, dumbo."

Stunned again, this time by her wacky reference, he

replies, "You know, no matter how sophisticated you think you've made yourself, you can't escape your left-coast sensibilities."

"This from the Great Midwesterner," she snorts. "Sorry. My inner Disney sort of came out."

"You should let it out more often. It's charming."

She isn't sure how to react to that. "We play at being worldly citizens, but we can't out grow our middle-class American roots, can we?" *Tim might as well be a dentist. I might as well be a checkout clerk at the hometown super market. I guess that's why I can't stay mad at him.*

He laughs. "How can you get so mad at me for being childish and foolish, when—"

Miko feels her own laughter bubbling up. She couldn't stop it.

Tim leans in, still giggling and their mouths meet with no laughter at all. They hold each other, tasting, hugging, and then grabbing at each other's clothing.

"Repeat after me," he says. "My door is always open."

She pulls back, retorting, ""I'm not saying that…like last time."

Laugh lines appear around his eyes. "Well, you can't blame a guy for trying."

She lets herself be pulled into his arms again. "Believe me, Cross. You are very trying."

He kisses her again, deeply, while fumbling with the clasp at the back of her bra. "I try. I try."

"No pressure, but—" Miko gasps, urgently. "—tick, tock."

"Okay, all ready," he answers from the side of his mouth. "Stop yelling, dammit!" And he lifts her off her feet and carries her to the cabin's soft bunk.

Afterward, they lie together. Tim drifts off to a peaceful sleep, while Miko watches the shadows from the curtains shift across the bulkheads and overhead. She is happy, yet concerned about what will happen now that her feelings have shifted back to Tim. Will she be able to hide it from Birol? *Is my life about to change again?*

Tim snores softly at her side. The sudden urge to smoke a cigarette makes her get up carefully and step naked to the open porthole to gaze at the distant stars and the sparkle of the sea.

It would be good to start over again. She imagines herself with Tim skimming along on some swift sailboat as it cleaves the waves and the wind. He would steer her safely back into the harbor where they would walk along a sandy beach, shoes dangling from their hands.

Miko turns from the fluttering curtains and looks back at him. He is sitting up now on the edge of the bed. He holds an arm out to her. She comes to him in quiet acceptance, tousling his orange hair and pressing her face into his bare chest.

⌘⌘⌘

Sandrine sits on Birol's lap, nibbling his left ear. "You have finally overcome the 'Merchant of Death' label that so many of the news organizations have hung on you."

She shifts position and looks into his eyes. *Clouded gray like melted snow.*

"I'm a great admirer of Alfred Nobel," he says. "And I've used my position and fortune to promote peace."

They are wolves' eye. Like the wolves my father once hunted in the Alps.

"Once again I have the opportunity for greatness," he admits. "If I can manage the others and their actions, I can get everything I ever imagined. I'll have all the admiration I'll need."

A chill creeps up her bare spine. "And we can re-shape the world if you play your cards right."

"Cards." The word hangs on his lips for a second. "A fortuneteller once read my destiny in the cards. She told me not to let anything or anyone get in my way."

"I'll tell you your true fortune." Sandrine shifts position again, offering him her breasts. "You become the new Suleiman of a next Ottoman Empire. And any attempt to stop you will be met by your crushing, devastating force."

His hands slide up to grasp her. "Exactly."

❧❧❧

"Can I get you anything else?" Gi-cho hands Tim a glass of iced vodka.

He takes a sip of the clear burning liquid and lets his mind wander. *She's certainly attractive, and her attention is flattering, but—*

The young, diminutive Korean woman sits next to him at the bar in the ship's lounge.

—but, ultimately my feelings for her are only a fling. I'm looking for something lasting, and it's hard to get over your first love.

He finds himself imagining Miko in his arms again. Her fawn hair, her hazel eyes, her sweet-smelling soft skin. "No." He smiles weakly. "I guess that will be all."

CHAPTER 29

The word has gone out to all the sports networks—soccer, tennis, baseball, even golf. Major political parties in major countries have been notified. Music fans, government agencies, universities, schools, and retirement communities have agreed to cooperate. All media, electronic, audio and video have been alerted and brought on board with the program.

"Is everyone covered? Did you double check?"

Tim tries to assure her. "Yes, Mik, we got full confirmation from all the sports networks. They're spreading the word."

"Louis. What have we forgotten? The music broadcasts?"

"Relax, will you, Miko? Haven't you heard their constant promos?"

"I guess. But, still…"

Everyone from all the sources is scheduled to begin

transmitting at midnight GMT worldwide. The key is to continue sending the proscribed frequency into every corner of the globe for at least an hour. Cellphones tap into the pulsing signal and are held high on rooftops and even street corners in hundreds of small towns and cities.

The celebrities who have made the joint announcement continue to promote the activity—almost bragging. Listeners and viewers contribute their signal into the unified force that spreads throughout the atmosphere.

ନ୍ତ୍ର

"Sometimes I just do not understand you, Miko." Louis is scanning a stream of data as it scrolls down a computer screen. "He's a great guy, and I know you two used to have something together. Something a lot more than just a working relationship."

"If you think he's such a great catch," Miko sniffs, "you should go after him yourself."

"Don't think I haven't thought about it."

"What did he say?"

"He hasn't a clue," the Navajo replies, ruefully. "Besides, he's all wrapped up with you. Do you know, he once told me he remembered which earrings you were wearing? Now if that doesn't mean he cares deeply for you, I don't know want does."

She touches the side of her head, below her ear. There is no jewelry there now, but the thought that he's noticed has taken her completely by surprise. *Maybe—no, that is silly. Isn't it?*

ᘐᗅᘐᗅ

Tim and Boyd sit at the bar with its rapidly dwindling alcoholic resources.

"I have to say," the reporter swirls the Jamaican rum in his glass, "this has been one hell of an adventure."

Boyd shuffles his deck of cards and observes, "I see that you're finally blending fiction with your factual reporting."

"You're right," Tim realizes. "At times, I *do* see some of this as if it were fiction. I think it's an acquired trait that has rubbed off from you."

"Ah, yes. But for the best of causes. Agreed?"

Tim doesn't know how to answer. He takes a swallow of tangy booze. "You know, I'm really sorry now for turning you in, boss. If I'd known then—"

"Don't let it bother you, son. I got over it years ago." Boyd casually taps the deck of cards on the counter top to create a tight packet and tucks them away into the pocket of his coat. "Prison can sometimes do that to a man— give him a perspective he never had before. In your mind, you must have thought you were doing what's right. Right?"

Tim is surprised that Boyd kows him so well. "Right, I guess." He laughs. "My dad never understood that about me."

"Many fathers are like that. Mine was—" The man coughs quietly. "Well, let's just say he wanted what he thought would be best for me. In the long run, he may have been right all along."

Tim blinks. "I don't follow. What did he want for you?"

A sudden rumbling sounds in the distance. Another quake shakes the area, sending gusts of smoke above the shoreline and making the yacht oscillate as if from a storm at sea.

Boyd smiles. "The adventure continues."

Tim grabs hold of the edge of the bar. *A spring has no power until it's compressed.*

⌘

Boyd hurries to check in with Louis for a status report on the latest unsettling quake activity.

The Navajo sits in front of his bank of computer screens and keyboards. He seems to have recovered well and is now in his element, sending and receiving messages and updates via a dozen different programs and accounts, while monitoring the progress of the Flashmob transmissions.

"How's it going, Featherstone?"

Louis looks up, but continues typing. *How does he do that?*

"Oh, so you have taken to using the name Tim calls me," the Navajo web-warrior observes. "That is good. It makes me feel more like part of the team."

"I'd say that right now," Boyd stifles a tickle in his throat, "you're the cornerstone."

"Or the anchor." Louis stops tapping the keyboard. "I know that I've been holding everyone down. And I dislike being the one who sits and waits for things to happen. The next time we go out on a case or caper or whatever you call it, I want to be active."

"I'm sorry that you were injured."

"Forget that. I am fit and fine. I heal quickly, un-like…" He lets the sentence trail away.

"You mean, unlike me?"

"Okay, okay. I went too far. Now I am the one who is sorry." He waves a hand as if to clear the air.

Boyd rests his own hand on Louis's shoulder. "I promise you that the next time we have to go out, you'll be part of the operation." *Assuming you feel up to it.*

"Thanks, boss." He touches a finger to his forehead in salute. "That means a lot to me."

Three different screens pop open video windows, and Louis goes back to monitoring the latest stage of the counter-frequency transmission and the effects of the recent quakes.

☙❧

Miko spreads her hands wide. "I just wanted to say that I'm profoundly impressed how well you've held it together."

Her grandiose comment stings Tim's ego, but he has to admit that she is basically correct. "Yeah," he drawls, "It's been tough on all of us. Hank and his new baby. Louis and his concussion. Jae Kim and his sister facing one medical emergency after another—"

"Uh…about Gi-cho. She strikes me as a very capable

and attractive addition to our crew, don't you think? A little young, but…"

She is fishing for an emotional response from him. He rubs the stubble on his jaw warily. "Oh, we're a team again, now?"

That is not the response she had wanted. "I'd say that we've passed that point weeks ago. Wouldn't you?"

"I guess." He pours each of them a stiff shot of the last of the rum. "It feels great, doesn't it? Righting wrongs. Solving puzzles. Saving lives."

"Damn, Tim. You're such a boy scout! I know now that it's part of what attracted me to you back when we opened our agency together, but…"

"What do you mean?" He tilts back to get a good look at her expression. "You're the one who always wanted to seek out the truth. You once told me that you hated liars and people who weren't true to their—"

"Do you see it now?" Her eyes are appraising. "Do you see why I hated you for turning Boyd over to the police, back then?"

"Yeah. I get it now. How about you?"

"How about me what?"

"Do you get that I did it because he was lying to us about the true nature of our cause? He never told us the full story. Cripe! Sometimes I think he never will."

She folds her arms and stares at him with unconscious grace. "You're probably right. Even now, I have the feeling that he has an ulterior motive for getting us all back together again."

"He's always up to something. Why do we even trust him?"

Tim locates a new bottle in the back of the bar and carefully flows more whiskey into their glasses. "It's sort of perverse, isn't it? Sometimes we simply do things against our own best interests."

She lifts her chin defensively and elbows him. "Like drinking too much."

He looks at the amber fluid in his glass and then pours it into a cluttered trash can. "Yeah. Like drinking too much or holding a grudge too long."

Impressed, Miko dribbles her own drink into the waste can, mingling it with his. "Or avoiding the truth and fighting your own feelings about someone."

"God, I've missed you, Mik. Maybe I turned on Boyd 'cause I thought you were taken with him."

"Oh, so now it's my fault, huh?"

"No. The fault is clearly mine. I just mean, maybe I was afraid I was losing you to his suave, casual, confident manner."

"Well, he doesn't seem casual or very confident these days. Does he?"

"I know." Tim pinches the bridge of his nose. "He's hurting. I watched him manipulating those playing cards and saw the struggle growing on his face. He's an old man now. And, unlike us, his best days are behind him."

"Our best days are here now," Miko says. "And we should make the best of them."

He studies her disturbing hazel eyes. "It's all for the best." A small smile twists the side of his face.

"Best that you shut up, before I slap you one."

Together, they smile. "Best."

"Okay." He beams. "Best we get back to work."

CHAPTER 30

Despite the resonating effects of the flash-mob frequency, a shifting plate continues to grind itself into the Asian continent along the northern border of India. The worst results are felt throughout the many mouths of the Ganges River. Buildings topple in Dhaka, Rangpur and hundreds of smaller villages in Bangladesh. The seismic shocks ripple across Calcutta, almost hourly.

"I don't know how much more of this we can take."

"I know, Featherstone. I can't tell if it's getting better or worse."

"If the power keeps going out, we may never know."

The Earth only slowly begins to settle down. Fires break out on nearly every street around Birol's production facility. Car alarms blast, dogs shiver and bark, distant sirens moan and wail forlornly. Train tracks snap apart. Concrete cracks. Bridges tilt and tumble. Planes are grounded, and a thick, choking smoke rises to hover over the city.

The billionaire—if that term means anything any longer—is *not* secure in his position within the new world order. There is a very good chance that, as the quakes, riots, and destruction continue, soon there will be no order at all.

Birol's single hope to thrive under these conditions and take control rests on his ability to buy off his competitors and purchase their loyalty. To do this, he knows he is compelled to cash in the trove of art treasures he's stored away over the years. And to do that, he has to go where they are secretly and securely cached.

While the rest of the team monitors the successful influence of the flashed frequency from the control consul on Boyd's ship, Miko returns to shore to keep an eye on Birol. Her suspicions have grown, especially after he turned down her request to help generate the counter frequency. She is beginning to believe that he views the quakes as an opportunity to expand his influence in a crumbling world. *His goal has always been about gaining power. He takes and takes and never gives unless there's something massive to be gained.*

She knows he's recently aligned himself with the Russian Council. And she suspects that he still has vast wealth hidden somewhere, probably nearby, given the "shaky" conditions of the world market. *I'm certain he'll try to buy his way into a dictatorship.*

Miko is the team member closest to Birol and thus, in her mind, the best person to watch his actions and monitor his moves. She follows him from a distance, confident that he is not aware of her suspicions.

"Can you hear me?" She speaks quietly into the edge of her phone. "He's leaving his office without the usual security detail."

Tim's voice comes back to her. "Maybe he's going to take a leak."

She rolls her eyes. "He has his own washroom in his office, dummy. He's obviously headed somewhere special on his own."

"You following?"

"Like a lamb," she replies, "but not to slaughter. I know him too well."

"Just be careful."

The hallway floor beneath her feet shakes, as does the most of the building, from a minor trembler. A fluorescent tube falls from a light fixture behind her, exploding with a startling *pop*.

"Mik, you okay?" Tim asks urgently.

"Fine," she hisses. "I'm fine. Had the shit scared out of me for a second, is all. He's taking a flight of stairs I've never noticed before down below the ground floor."

"Keep talking, so I'll know that the signal still comes through when you're under ground."

"Roger, that. What should I talk about?"

"I don't know. The weather, sports, our relationship, your favorite song."

"Our relationship?" She starts down the stairway, one hand on the cold metal railing.

A nervous yawn escapes her lips. She can feel the

long hours catching up with her. *Brain's not working as fast as I'd like. Running on fumes.* "My mom used to sing this to me when I was little. 'The moon belongs to every-one. The best things in life are free. The stars belong to-'. Wait! Are you broadcasting this?"

"Um…no," Tim quickly sputters. "Not at all. Keep going."

She peers around a corner in a cement-block corridor and spies Birol standing before a reinforced doorway. He leans his head into an eye-level scanning device attached to the door. It appears to be a retinal security reader, but after several failed attempts, Birol curses and consults a mobile phone to manually key in a code sequence on the keypad beneath the scanner: *76395*.

Miko recites the numbers into her own phone, while from a distance, she watches Birol open the door and pass from view.

She cautiously dashes forward and keys in the same combination, hoping that it doesn't change on a pre-set basis. The door opens to her touch. After a glance back up and down the shadowy hallway, she goes through the entranceway to find another short hall that leads to a high-ceiling room crammed with crates and containers, heaps of ruddy gold coins and black-struck gilt lacquer on wood. *It's a locked storage room or warehouse. No, it's a vault!*

Ducking down behind a couple of wooden packing cases labeled "Tucker's Cross" and "Coronet of Lly-welyn ap Gruffudd," Miko watches Birol open a hinged shipping create. He reaches in, pushes back a cushion of excelsior and lifts an earthen amphora that has to be at least two thousand years old. The ancient clay jug splits apart in his large hands, spilling hundreds of gray metal disks to the floor in a clattering array. A few disks roll away to fall silent next to a necklace of what appear to be Solok rubies set in silver.

The billionaire's dry laugh blends with the sound of the coins rattling across the stone floor. The combined sound is so loud that Miko doesn't hear the soft footsteps behind her until an ice-cutting voice commands, *"Haut les mains, mon petit."*

⌘

Sandrine Lecombe boldly steps out from behind a Grecian statue of a proud warrior and levels the snout of a dark nine-millimeter Beretta pistol at Miko's breasts. The French woman lets a smile spread across his lips. *This time, I've got her cold and alone.*

Birol has instructed her to meet him here, but she never expected to find Miko trailing behind like a lost kitten. *Kitten my ass. She's a tiger. One that needs to be put down once and for all time.*

Sandrine watches as Miko walks backward, with hands raised, toward the spot where the round-faced billionaire stands holding a jewel-encrusted dagger. She smiles and listens while the blonde bitch pleads, "Do something, Birol. She has a gun on me."

The man says nothing, barely reacting.

"He doesn't hear you any longer, Miko," Sandrine

purrs, advancing. "I'm with him now, and he's with me."

"What does she mean?" Miko asks Birol's.

"I mean," Sandrine continues, pressing forward until the three of them are gathered close beside the pile of spilled coins, "that I've taken your place. I've proven my loyalty to him, while you have gone off to play with your little friends."

Miko utters a moan. "You're insane with jealousy and greed. What is all of this?" she asks, gesturing slightly to indicate the room's contents.

"This, my dear Miko," Birol answers, "is one of my basic resources. The biggest and best, I might add. The wealth of the collection you see here is ten times that of the vault you and your 'bishop' friends robbed years ago in Turkey. Even as the world outside crumbles, the value of these items remains high."

Miko tilts her head, almost defiantly, questioning, "And you'll use this loot to buy your way to some sort of empire?"

"Correction," Sandrine replies. "*We'll* use it for all that and much more. But you won't know when it happens because you're not leaving here alive. I'll see to that."

❦

"And I will see that you do nothing of the kind." Louis steps from a deep shadow next to the entrance of the chamber. His firm voice echoes of the vaulted ceiling. The gun in his fist feels warm and almost alive.

Despite his earlier injury and current circumstances, he is remarkably comfortable. No head pain—just a solid feeling of self-satisfaction that he is again playing an important role within the team. Tim and Boyd stand next to him, but *he* is the one with the firepower. He is the one in control. *My brother would be proud.*

If possible, Birol's eyes grew even larger. "How? How did you get here?"

Louis lets his grin widen. "Through the wonders of science."

"Miko's phone has been on the whole time," Tim adds, ruining the grandstand effect by giving away the secret truth.

Sandrine lowers her Beretta. Boyd is reaching to take it from her when a bucking quake shakes the floor and cascades chucks of the ceiling down on the room's shipping crates and helpless inhabitants.

A thunderous rumble and a thick mass of dust erupt into the air of the closed chamber. Stark terror lances up Louis's spine. The light in the room fades as a second shockwave shakes the vault and someone screams, "We'll be crushed in here!"

A heavy crossbeam tumbles from the ceiling. Louis hears it clatter and sees with horror that it comes to rest diagonally blocking the vault's entrance door. Through the cloud of dust, he shouts in his best military authoritarian voice, "We have to work together to move out of here." Someone coughs behind him.

It sounds like a man choking on the filth in the air.

Abruptly, through the settling haze, he begins to

make out the form of Birol staggering toward him. The rich man's body is bent slightly from weakness or fatigue.

Still holding his gun, Louis comes forward to help the man. "Here," he says. "We're over here."

Birol glares up at him, carrying something in his right hand. *Shit! Now* he *has a gun.*

Louis reaches for the weapon, but Birol fires. Twice.

A stunning impact catches Louis in the chest. He tries to breathe. Fear like wildfire courses through his body. He comes down on one knee, striking his head on the side of an oaken crate. Darkness swarms. Someone calls to him from a distance. He opens his mouth to answer, but no sound will come out. The darkness thickens around him, gathering him up and carrying him off to…

☙☙☙

Tim shouts to his fallen friend, seeing him slump between two shipping containers. He rushes past Bronze Age and Byzantine era sculptures. Already, a deep red stain spreads across Louis's chest. Tim presses his palm over the bullet wound. *Stop the blood. Stop the blood.*

The prostrate Louis screams from the pressure and Tim yanks his dripping hand back. *Dripping with blood.*

A breath blows past Tim's face and the Navajo slumps, unmoving. "No. Featherstone. Stay with me! God, don't you die."

Boyd and Miko come back from the blocked entrance to stand over the Tim and the body.

"Is he dead?" The question rattles from where Birol stands several feet away. "Did I kill him?"

A blistering rage explodes inside Tim. "You god-dammed sonofabitch!" His throat aches.

Boyd and Miko grab and hold him, forcing him away from the point of Birol's deadly handgun.

For the first time since the aftershock, Sandrine comes into view. She tosses her head, flipping her red hair away from her left cheek. She too carries a firearm. "Drop your weapons," the woman commands, moving to stand near the billionaire.

Tim seriously calculates shaking off the hands that hold him and firing his automatic regardless of conse-quences.

Boyd tosses his gun behind a Ming-glazed urn that has miraculously remained un-damaged until the discard-ed weapon bounces and shatters the base of the vessel that tilts and crashes into a thousand and one pieces.

Tim cannot help thinking, *That's pretty cute.* He lets out a chuckle that relieves a portion of the tension in his muscles and throws his gun up and out into the dusty darkness. *Maybe I'll hit something extremely valuable.*

Sandrine watches the firearm sail away and then turns back to face him.

Tim clinches his jaw and again looks down at the fallen Indian.

"Now comes the good part," Sandrine gloats.

"What happened to you?" Tim asks her, simply. "You used to be one of us."

⌀⌀⌀

The words sting her more than she'd expected. Sandrine takes in a deep breath to steady her nerves. "What happened?" She trains her nine-millimeter automatic on Miko's head. "She happened. That's what."

Without hesitation, she feels the satisfaction of pulling the Beretta's trigger.

The bullet speeds past Miko, nicking her left earlobe.

"Christ!" Miko screams, clutching the side of her head with both hands to stench the bleeding. "You almost killed me, you bitch!"

Sandrine cackles with obvious delight and glanced at Birol. The barrel of the billionaire's gun is pointed directly at her.

Sandrine freezes. "No. Not me." Her face becomes flushed and pleading. Her eyes widen in abject fear.

"No one shoots the woman I love."

Sandrine hears both bullets strike her brain. She hears a shrill scream. She hears distant music. She hears her mother call her name. She hears what sounds like the roar of the ocean and then…nothing.

⁓⊃⁓⊃

Boyd sees Sandrine's body shudder and slump forward. Then the redhead staggers back, her face a mask of surprise. She leans to one side, falling over and down into a silent heap.

He hears Miko cry emphatically, "I'll never be yours again."

Tim is wrapping his arms around Miko, snuggling

her head. She doesn't seem seriously injured. Birol just stands there, accepting the insult, but still holding the gun.

I have to find a way to stop this mad man. Making a gesture with his hand for the couple to stand back, Boyd rises to his full height. "So this is it?" he asks. "We finally face off, man against man." *And I'm under the ground again, just like back in that Turkish hell hole.*

Birol gives a satisfied grunt. "Except, that I'm the only one with a weapon."

Boyd struggles to keep his voice calm. "If you'll allow me." Slowly, he reaches into the inside breast pocket of his coat and brings out a deck of playing cards.

With his distended eyes, Birol watches as the deck is fanned. *His pride is keeping him from firing on me,* Boyd tells himself. *His curiosity might let me get the upper hand.*

In a rapid flurry of riffs and almost hypnotic skill of cardisty, Boyd cuts the deck and fans the cards with his fingertips. He again cuts the results and fans them once more. Cutting, fanning, building an actual house of cards in the air before his chest.

He keeps manipulating smaller and smaller stacks of cards on the tips of his fingers, flourishing them in an artistic display of skillful dexterity. Birol seems captivated, until the split second when Boyd shoots the King of Hearts and then the Ace of Spades in the direction of the billionaire's bulging eyes.

Just at the moment when the cards bullet from Boyd's hands, a sharp arthritic pain pierces his thumb, sending the cards spiraling past Birol's head to clatter and fall flat into the darkness. The rest of the deck spills from his fingers and flutters to the floor.

ფფ

Birol has had enough of this picturesque outlaw and his petty gang. These people have broken in here, planning to rob him. Again. And Miko now has rejected him, once and for all, while that young man at her side has obviously won her heart. Now, this decrepit thief has tried and failed to win their long-standing duel with his pathetic, inept card trick. *This ends now.*

Reaching with his left hand, Birol picks up a ruby-encrusted rapier, while keeping a firm grip on the gun in his right fist. "As I recall," he says, directing his words at Boyd, "you used to be quite a good swordsman."

Boyd offers the slightest of shrugs. "An affectation of my youth, I'm afraid. It came from watching too many roguish adventures on television."

Birol shakes his head in distain. *I've waited a long time to put an end to this fool.* He tosses the dueling sword aside, like a toy and moves forward. "And now I have you where you cannot run away to fight again." The words feel warm on his lips and delicious on his tongue. "After I've killed you, Boyd, I'll shoot the two lovers."

His opponent stands there speechless, head slightly bowed, body bent from the hips, as if contrite, accepting his fate.

Birol aims the weapon directly between Boyd's eyes.

Then his own eyes burst from his head as a thirty-ounce lead bullet blasts the side of his round, bald skull and drills through his brain.

෮෩෮෩

Both Tim and Miko shout at the man lying at their feet. "Louis!" The smoking gun at his hand clatters to the concrete. A smile seems to appear on his lips.

Tim tries to find signs of a pulse, but there is none. He looks up at Miko, who still holds her hand against the side of her head. "He's gone."

"Are you sure?"

Boyd comes over and places two fingertips next to the Navajo's throat. No one dares breathe. Boyd sighs. "I'm afraid, this time he's gone for good."

Above their heads, a creaking noise rolls across the vault. A stream of dirt and cement dust flows down covering a pile of papyrus scrolls.

"We still have to get out of here," Miko warned, "before the ceiling caves in."

Boyd steps back a pace and scans the room. "Let's see if we can move that metal beam blocking the door."

Tim wipes his hands on his knees. "What about Louis?"

"Let's get out of here first," Miko reasons. "Then we can come back for his body."

The three stumble over the rubble that blankets the remaining treasures housed in the vault. Tim hopes no new quakes will hit. Miko begins to feel dizzy from loss of blood or the shock of being nearly shot in the head.

Bending their collective backs to the task, they manage to heave the beam off center enough to wedge one at a time through the crack in the doorway.

Miko makes it through first and immediately starts leading the way up the corridor to the stairs. Tim eases past next, following her.

Once they reach it to the ground floor, she stumbles again and finds that Boyd is not with them. "Where is he?"

Tim growls deep in his throat and shakes his fists. "He must have gone back for Louis."

"Or he had another seizure," she cries.

The earth trembles again. They clutch hold of the stairway railing as an enormous cloud of dust and foul air billows up past.

"I'm going back for him," Miko says.

Tim grasps her wrist. "No. He's gone."

"No, he's not."

"He's Boyd. And we have to take care of ourselves."

"He's Boyd," she repeats, feeling a dizzying wave wash over her again.

"Look at you. You're hurt and need Kim's medical attention."

"But…" She is confused and torn. *I don't…don't know what to do.*

"Miko. It's the right thing to do. Come on."

The ground shakes again as if to remind her of their danger.

She turns, dazed by events, and accepts Tim's authoritativeness, following him into the sunlight, while repeating, "He's Boyd."

EPILOGUE

Monday, August 10, 2020, Everywhere:

The quakes lessen gradually over the ensuing weeks until the planet settles back into a relatively quiet state.

But the world at large is still a mess. Between the effects of the virus and the shaking of the landmasses, it will be at least a half decade before life gets back to what most people remember as "normal." And that is only if no new diseases, from the lack of clean water, or new wars, from lack of fresh food, threaten to send mankind back down into a death-spiral.

It will be hard on everyone for a time, but the Western Hemisphere is already rebounding. Europe has survived with only moderate loses. Asia and Australia can already be seen as robust enough to handle anything new thrown at them. Only Africa and Russia labor under the terrible strain of the combined catastrophes. The rest of the world has already set programs into motion to help heal the terrible losses.

Hank, his wife, and son convert the *Blue Trane* bar into a restaurant to help feed the needy.

Kim goes back to support his family in Korea.

Hammer returns to managing a task force at Europol.

Tim and Miko decide to re-open their investigations agency again, helping to track down loved ones. This time, she will take charge of picking their cases, and he will take charge of his sobriety. Tim is just happy to have her back.

On the northern coast of Turkey, a cherry-red Skycar circles the ruins of Birol's estate. Finding a clear patch of land in which to set down, the pilot shifts the rotors of the small VTOL vehicle and soon climbs out to search among the massive granite pile that was once a regal mansion facing the Black Sea. Now among the ominous ruins, the figure in the flight suit consults a diagram of the surrounding area, displayed on a palm-sized computer tablet.

A swampy bitter odor, reminiscent of kimchee, rises from the greenish-brown surface of the nearby shore. The sinking sun stabs the fading sky with bolts of pink and orange. No one comes to greet or confront the intruder.

The pilot approaches what appears to be a solid concrete wall. A dust-covered fire detector is mounted there. The intruder tugs on the circular device which swings outward, exposing a keypad. A gloved hand enters *BZK76395* and hidden motors thrum to life retracting a portion of the wall to one side and creating an opening.

Cobwebs hang from the dark chamber's ceiling, and rat droppings litter the floor. The musty air smells of decay and mold. From the confused rubble, a brass and tin container comes to the surface. It is a perfect cube, empty but inscribed with exotic characters. The intruder ignores the dusty and tattered Nazi relics. *Priceless, but disgusting.*

Tapping the com icon to access a secured phone line, the pilot struggles to avoid a note of triumph. "I have the box that once housed the Pandora Block, and the inscription on it appears to be just as you suspected."

A wavering, electronic voice comes back. "Excellent."

"This might be the clue to the cure that you need. Looks like you'll live to fight another day, boss."

Boyd responds from far away, where he lies convalescing. "Thank you, Gi-cho. It's been fun, and you're a good little thief."

The Skycar soon rises, adjusting the tilt of its engines to soar into the pink and orange sherbet sunset.

END

The Facts Behind the Fiction

Russian A-Bomb Detection: In 1949, the US needed to know if the Russians truly had the A-bomb. Since the USSR was so vast, the only effective way to test for results of a detonation was to "sniff" the air for signs of radioactive particles drifting across the Pacific Ocean or, even better, above Russia itself.

Skycar: A number of companies have actual working models of this vehicle in various forms, the most popular being Terrafugia's TF-X, Joby Aviation's "drone airplane" and Moller's Skycar. The cascade vane systems on the engines of the latter, alter their thrust through duct exits, allowing the craft to come to a complete stop and hover before descending and lightly setting down.

Lost Treasure: The coronet of Llywelyn ap Gruffudd, the last king of Wales, was seized in 1284 along with other holy artefacts and taken to Westminster Abbey in London until stolen in 1303 and remains unaccounted for. The heavily-jeweled insignia of the Most Illustrious Order of St. Patrick was stolen from Dublin Castle in 1907. The emerald-studded Tucker's Cross, discovered in a shipwreck in 1955, was stolen from a museum in Bermuda in 1959.

SpaceX: Elon Musk's otherworldly adventure begins with a series of successful launches and landings of two-stage vehicles powered by liquid oxygen (LOX) and rocket-grade kerosene (RP-1). Recovery systems stationed on platforms floating at sea allow the return and intact recovery of first-stage sections with their Merlin engines.

Drones and Condors: The United States military is only one organization that trains large birds of prey like eagles and falcons to bring down remote-controlled aircraft. The concept was first successfully employed by police in the Netherlands in 2015.

Microwave Resonant Absorption (MAR): Dual frequencies of the first and eleventh harmonic have been proposed for years to destroy cancer cells. In vitro, resonating microwaves can be absorbed by certain types of viruses without damage to living tissue, as outlined in the December 2016 scientific report in Nature which references the US patent for constructing such a device.

Uncle Albert: The first person to navigate by air from the west coast to Hawaii, US Air Force General Albert F. Hegenberger commanded the US Air Force Office of Atomic Energy (AFOAT) a group whose work remained top secret until the 1980s. In 1949, he informed President Truman of the successful detection of radioactive particles above Soviet airspace. Earlier in 1947, from Holloman AFB, he sent microphones up in high-altitude balloons to detect atomic blasts; one of these unidentified flying objects crashed and was quickly whisked away from nearby Roswell, New Mexico. And, yes, he was the author's uncle.

About the Author

John Hegenberger writes adventure, mystery, science, and horror fiction. Born and raised in the heart of the heartland, Columbus, Ohio, he is the author of Tripleye series and the Stan Wade LAPI series from Black Opal Books. Father of three, a tennis enthusiast, collector of silent films and OTR, hiker, Francophile, B.A. Comparative Literature, ex-navy, ex-comic book dealer, ex-marketing exec at Exxon, AT&T, and IBM, he has been happily married forty-eight years.

Over the years, he's published two non-fiction books about collecting pop-culture movie memorabilia and comic books and sold half a dozen stories to magazines and anthologies. Follow his adventures at johnhegenberger.com and have fun.